THE BOBBSEY TWINS
AND THE MYSTERY AT SNOW LODGE

The Bobbsey Twins and the Mystery at Snow Lodge

By

LAURA LEE HOPE

GROSSET & DUNLAP
Publishers   *New York*

The Bobbsey Twins and the Mystery at Snow Lodge

CONTENTS

THE BOBBSEY TWINS
AND THE MYSTERY AT SNOW LODGE

CHAPTER I

RUNAWAY HORSE

"WOW! Look at this snowdrift, Flossie!" exclaimed six-year-old Freddie Bobbsey, peering over the porch railing of their home.

"Oh, let's play in it!" his sister suggested.

The golden-haired, six-year-old twins exchanged mischievous glances, their blue eyes dancing with excitement.

"Last one in is a turkey!" Freddie shouted, climbing onto the low railing. He stood atop it for a moment, balancing unsteadily while Flossie scrambled up. But she was too late.

With a cry of, "You're the turkey, Floss!" he plunged feet first into the fluffy white mass and disappeared!

Flossie jumped in after her twin, holding her nose and shutting her eyes tight. Quickly Freddie scrambled out of the drift, laughing and blowing snowflakes from his face. Then Flossie followed, shaking the snow from her curls.

1

As Freddie packed a snowball, Flossie sneaked past him, crying, "I'll bet I'll beat you this time!"

Flossie raced up the front porch steps of the comfortable, rambling house. Climbing onto the railing again, she was about to plunge into the drift when she saw that Freddie was still standing where she had left him.

"Wait, Flossie!" cried her twin, cocking his head to the right. He was listening to a jingling sound which cut through the frosty morning air.

"Oh, sleigh bells!" Flossie exclaimed.

The noise grew louder. A moment later they saw a jet-black horse drawing an old-fashioned sleigh trotting down the street. The sleigh was full of gift-wrapped packages.

An elderly man in a heavy red jacket, but no hat, sat very erect on the front seat, holding the reins to which sleigh bells were attached.

"Santa Claus!" Freddie cried, as the wind blew the man's white hair in a cloud about his head.

The sleigh had a high, curved back and low sides. In contrast to its black body the seat upholstery and runners were a bright red.

Freddie and Flossie, curious to see where it was going, ran down the walk of their home and along the street. Halfway down the block the driver reined in and stopped before a house. He selected several packages from the rear of the sleigh and went around to the back door.

"This is really like Christmas," said Flossie. She counted on her fingers. "And it's only one week off!"

Freddie grinned. "Not even one whole week of school!" he said.

The little boy had not taken his eyes from the coal-black mare standing near the curb. The horse was pawing the snow and tossing her head as if she were impatient to be off. Suddenly a snowball whizzed through the air and hit the horse *bang* on the side of the head. She whinnied loudly, then with a jerk started off down the street.

"She's running away!" cried Freddie excitedly.

The small twins started after the horse, yelling, "Whoa! Whoa!"

The animal paid no attention. Other children playing on their lawns and a couple of women along the street also called to the horse. But she did not stop.

"She'll—she'll run into somebody!" Flossie gasped worriedly.

At this very moment they saw three children coming up the street. "Bert and Nan, and Charlie Mason!" Freddie exclaimed. Bert and Nan were the twelve-year-old Bobbsey twins. Charlie Mason was Bert's best friend.

"Oh, look!" Flossie yelled. "Oh!"

Charlie and Bert had run out into the street and were dancing around, waving their arms wildly, trying to stop the horse. The animal zigzagged from side to side and slowed down but did not stop.

Flossie, terrified now, put her hands over her

eyes and refused to look. But Freddie watched the scene in fascination. Bert and Charlie separated, one going to each side of the runaway horse. Each grabbed the bridle strap near the bit and hung on. First they would run a few steps, then swing their feet up off the snow, putting their full weight on the horse's bit.

"Whoa! Whoa!" Bert kept yelling.

The pull on the animal's mouth hurt her very much, and it was not long before she stopped running. Bert now jumped into the sleigh, and Charlie threw him the reins, which were dragging on the ground.

"Oh, boys, that was terrific!" Nan Bobbsey exclaimed, rushing up. The slim, dark-haired, brown-eyed girl began to stroke the horse's head, and in a short while the animal was quiet.

At that moment there was a worried shout from down the street, and the white-haired sleigh owner rushed up.

"What's going on here?" he cried. "What happened to Daisy?"

Everyone talked at once, and the owner of the horse and sleigh looked confused. But gradually the story was pieced together.

The man nodded his head sharply, then turned to Bert, who stepped from the sleigh. "You stopped Daisy, did you?" he said.

"Charlie and I, yes, sir," was the answer.

The elderly man hesitated a moment, his

pale blue eyes staring intently at Bert. "I've seen you around Lakeport before," he finally said. "Your name is—"

"Bert Bobbsey."

"*Richard Bobbsey's son?*"

Bert nodded proudly and introduced Nan and the smaller twins.

The man walked toward his sleigh, then turned again to the children. "You know," he mused, "it's been five years since a Bobbsey has come into my life. Yet today the Bobbseys have done me a favor for the second time."

Nan and Bert exchanged puzzled glances, as the owner added, "Wonder if this'll be the last time, or—"

"I beg your pardon, sir?" Bert queried.

"What for?" was the blunt return.

Bert flushed. "I mean I don't understand. You said it's been five years—"

"Yes, yes," the man muttered. "But forget I said that." A sad, thoughtful look crossed his seamed face.

Nan glanced at Bert. "Why is he acting so mysterious?" she thought.

Bert shook his head, thinking, "I wonder why he drives that old-fashioned sleigh? And why does he look so sad at times?"

Freddie was more blunt and said aloud, "You're a mystery Santa Claus. Why?"

At this the man threw back his head and

laughed. "Oh, not so mysterious," he said. "I just like to exercise Daisy, and it's fun delivering Christmas packages this way."

Still the old gentleman did not give his name. Instead, he put his hands on Bert's and Charlie's shoulders and said:

"Forgive me. I haven't properly thanked you boys for stopping Daisy. It was a brave thing to do, and I want you to have this."

He pulled a crumpled piece of paper from his pocket and slipped it into Bert's hand, then turned away and climbed into his sleigh.

Opening his hand, Bert spread out the piece of paper. *It was a five-dollar bill!*

Charlie and the Bobbseys gasped. Quickly Bert called to the old gentleman who had gathered the reins and was about to drive away.

"Wait, sir! We can't accept this," he cried. "We were glad we could stop your horse."

"That's all right," was the reply. A twinkle came into the man's penetrating eyes. "If you can't accept it for yourself, use the money for a Christmas treat for your friends."

"Well, in that case," Bert said, smiling, "we'll be glad to accept it. Thanks very much, Mr.— er—"

But Bert's attempt to learn the old gentleman's name met with no success. Either the man had not heard or did not wish to tell his name, for he shook the reins sharply and sped off.

"Well, can you beat that!" Charlie Mason exclaimed. "Does anyone know who he is?"

"I do," said a young woman standing nearby. "That's Jess Carford. He owns Snow Lodge, at the other end of Lake Metoka."

Nan asked if she knew why Mr. Carford drove the old-fashioned sleigh. "Yes," she said. "During the Christmas season Mr. Carford uses it to deliver toys and candy to certain children in Lakeport who are less fortunate than others. He has done it every year since I can remember."

"Then he is a kind of Santa Claus," Flossie spoke up. "But why does he look so sad sometimes?"

The young woman hesitated a moment, then replied, "I was told that there was some mystery in connection with Snow Lodge. I know Mr. Carford doesn't live there now. But I've never heard why."

At the mention of a mystery, the four Bobbseys exchanged glances. Here was exciting news!

The twins hurried home, thinking their mother could explain the mystery. Reaching the house, they learned that Mr. Bobbsey had phoned from his office that he had been called away on a business trip. The twins' father owned a large lumberyard located on the shore of Lake Metoka. He frequently went out of town to purchase lumber.

"But Daddy will be home for Christmas next

week, won't he?" Flossie asked worriedly.

"Yes, indeed," replied the pretty mother of the four children.

Bert told her about Mr. Carford, but she knew little more than they had already heard. She did say, however, that she thought the mystery in connection with Snow Lodge concerned Mr. Carford's family.

"Perhaps he doesn't want to talk about it," Mrs. Bobbsey added gravely. "If you see him again, I think it would be best not to mention it unless he does."

In a little while Dinah, the jolly colored woman who helped Mrs. Bobbsey with the house work, announced that lunch was ready. Dinah and Sam, her husband, who drove a truck at the lumberyard, had had rooms on the third floor ever since the twins could remember. The whole family was very fond of the couple.

"Chicken soup with rice, and biscuits to go with it," said Dinah with a grin.

"Whoopee!" cried Freddie.

The children hurried to wash their hands, then went to the table. An hour later they asked their mother's permission to go coasting on the park hill.

"Go ahead, but dress warmly," she said.

A little later, the four Bobbseys were climbing King's Hill, a long, steep slope located on the outskirts of town.

"Crowded today, isn't it?" Nan remarked as a group of children on sleds, skis, and toboggans whizzed past them on the downward slope.

"Oh-oh, here comes Danny Rugg on that flashy new toboggan of his," said Bert.

"He must have a million boys on that thing!" Freddie exclaimed.

"Gracious, he's steering it this way, and all the boys are leaning to the left," Nan said in alarm. "Let's get out of the way!"

"And fast," said Bert.

Freddie, several yards away, had kneeled down to refasten the buckle on his snow boot and had not heard Bert's warning.

"Freddie! Freddie!" Nan called. "Watch out!"

The small boy looked up just in time to see the toboggan racing toward him.

CHAPTER II

THE SNOW BATTLE

DROPPING his sled rope, Freddie scampered out of the path of the speeding toboggan.

At the last possible moment, however, Danny and his friends leaned to the right and sent the toboggan careening past Freddie, showering him with a fine spray of snow.

Nan's brown eyes were snapping. "Danny may only have been fooling, but he could easily have misjudged the turn."

Her twin nodded grimly. This was not the first time that Danny Rugg, a schoolmate and bully, had tried to pull a mean trick on the Bobbseys. Aloud Bert said, "You were lucky, Freddie. Just the same, I'm going to have it out with Danny."

"Do it later," Nan urged. "Right now let's go coasting. Race you all down the hill!"

For the next half-hour the four children had a wonderful time. Then, while Flossie and Freddie took a little rest and Nan joined some of her girl chums coasting down the hill, Bert sought out Danny.

The bully had just climbed a little way up the slope when Bert walked over to him and stopped.

"Danny, you'd better be more careful with your steering and not scare other children the way you scared Freddie," he said sternly.

"Is that so?" jeered the bully. "Who do you think you are—a policeman?"

"No, I don't," Bert said firmly, doubling his fists. "But we're going to need one around here if you don't keep out of other people's way."

Danny started to laugh, but then, catching sight of the threatening look on Bert's face, backed away. "Okay, okay, can't you take a joke?"

Just then Charlie Mason walked up. "Hey, Bert, how about spending Mr. Carford's money now?"

Bert agreed, and the two boys collected a group of their friends. With whoops of joy, the children started off toward the center of town. Their destination was Jenkins' soda shop. Freddie arrived first and scrambled up on one of the high stools at the counter.

"About a hundred hot chocolates, please!" he said to the teen-aged clerk facing him.

"A hundred—" the startled youth began, but just then the rest of the children arrived.

Bert made an accurate count, and the clerk was relieved to learn that only twenty-four cups were required. Even so, he had his hands full for several minutes.

The steaming cups of hot chocolate, topped with whipped cream, were delicious. When the last drop had disappeared, all the children headed for home.

The next day was Sunday. After church and dinner, Bert and three of his chums decided to build a snow fort in a vacant lot near his father's lumberyard. The winter sunshine had started to melt the snow around town, but out by the lake it was still plentiful.

Just as they had completed the structure, Danny Rugg and several friends strolled up and ordered them out of it.

"I'm taking over here now," he bragged.

Bert refused to be bullied. "We built this fort and we're staying here," he said firmly.

That was all the excuse Danny needed to start a fight. "Okay, gang!" he cried. "Let's drive 'em out!"

The snow battle was on! Danny's friends took cover behind nearby trees and began peppering the fort with snowballs.

Bert motioned his chums to duck below the

walls, then whispered instructions. The boys fell to work and soon had a stockpile of snowballs.

Since they did not start fighting at once, Danny became over-confident. He stepped from behind the tree and beckoned to his friends.

"Come on, let's capture the fort from those sissies!" he called out.

At this Bert and his pals grinned at one another. They waited until the bully's gang drew nearer, then at the last minute, Bert yelled:

"Fire!"

Following Bert's command, a hail of snow-balls descended on the startled attackers. They staggered back, throwing up their arms in vain attempts to ward off the missiles.

Danny yelled a frantic order, and his pals retreated, then huddled together just out of firing range. There was silence.

"Look out for Danny, fellows," Bert warned his chums as he packed a snowball. "He's up to some trick!"

Several tense moments passed with the fort defenders stockpiling snowballs for the attack they knew would come. More snow was packed against the thick, four-foot-high walls. At last Bert's group was well prepared.

Suddenly Danny left his huddled group of buddies and waved a white handkerchief tied to a branch. He walked toward the fort slowly with his gang spread out in a semicircle behind him.

"They're surrendering!" Charlie Mason exclaimed, pounding Bert on the shoulder happily. "We've won!"

Charlie leaped to his feet. In that instant, a volley of snowballs filled the air. *Splat!* One struck Charlie squarely in the chest with such force that he staggered back and fell flat.

"Down! Everybody down!" Bert yelled. He crawled over to his stricken friend. "Are you okay, Charlie?"

"I—I guess so," was the gasping reply. "Just

knocked the wind out of me for a second."

"What a sly trick!" one of the other defenders exclaimed in disgust. "While Danny's waving a flag of truce, his buddies attack."

Bert examined the hard ball of snow which had hit Charlie. "Fellows, look!" he cried in amazement. "There's a stone in the center of this!"

"No wonder it hurt!" Charlie remarked, rubbing the sore spot.

Bert's fist pounded the snow. "That does it!" he yelled. "Let's teach those guys a lesson!"

Quickly the four boys stuffed snowballs inside their jackets and into pockets. With Bert in the lead they raced out of the fort and toward the trees where Danny had retreated with his gang after the sneak attack.

The next few minutes passed in a flash. Snowballs pelted Danny and his pals from everywhere, and the trees they tried to hide behind were no protection from the furious barrage.

At last, spattered with snow from head to foot, the boys in Danny's group fell back, then ran off in confusion.

Bert's attack had been a complete success!

Danny turned, just outside of firing range, and shook a threatening fist at him. "I'll get you, Bert Bobbsey!" he threatened. "You'll be sorry for this!"

"You're a poor sport, Danny," Charlie derided

the bully. "We beat you fairly—and without using stones either!" he added.

Red-faced and angrier than ever, the mean boy again shook his fist, then turned and raced off.

"Hey!" Bert exclaimed. "It's after five o'clock, fellows. Guess we'd better head for home."

The boys called good night to one another and started off toward their own homes. The skies had grown dark and a few soft white flakes had begun to fall.

Bert walked rapidly. Removing his gloves, he blew on his icy fingers. "It's grown a lot colder," he thought. "And these wet gloves don't help a bit. Boy, will I be glad to get home!"

Bert stepped up his pace and was just crossing Main Street when a car pulled up beside him.

"Hop in, son," a man's voice called. "It's too cold to walk far on a night like this!"

Bert peered into the car. The instrument panel lights revealed the white hair and lined face of Mr. Carford. "Why, thanks," Bert replied. "I would appreciate a lift."

He started to step into the car when suddenly his foot slipped on the icy curb. With a startled cry, the boy plunged face down onto the car seat.

"Whoa there, young fellow," said Mr. Carford. "Not hurt, are you?"

"No," Bert answered as he righted himself. Then he patted the seat and felt around on the floorboards of the car.

"Lose something?" Mr. Carford asked.

"I thought I heard something fall out of my pocket," said Bert. "Guess not, though. I have my wallet, and there isn't anything on the floor or seat."

They started off toward the Bobbsey home. Mr. Carford spoke about his horse Daisy and told Bert how fond he was of her. "It isn't often she runs away as she did yesterday," he commented.

Bert wanted to ask his new friend about the mystery at Snow Lodge, but remembering his mother's advice, he said nothing. Soon they drove up in front of the Bobbsey house where the boy thanked the elderly man, then jumped out.

Freddie and Flossie met him at the front door. The youngsters were dressed in snowsuits, hats, scarves, and mittens.

"Going out coasting in the dark?" Bert asked, giving Freddie a playful poke.

"No, we're trying to keep warm in here!" Freddie exclaimed. "It's freezing. Come in and see for yourself!"

When they went into the living room Mrs. Bobbsey explained that the furnace was not working. "The repairmen are in the basement now trying to fix it," she added.

Just as Bert finished telling his mother and Nan and the small twins about the snow fort fight, one of the workmen came up the basement steps. Stripping off his work gloves, he said:

"I'm afraid I have bad news for you, Mrs. Bobbsey. The furnace is in need of a major part. In fact, I'd strongly advise that you get a new furnace."

The children's mother looked worried. "But wouldn't a job like that take several days?"

"Yes, and with Christmas coming up the end of the week, the job would take longer."

"What would we do for heat in the meantime?" Mrs. Bobbsey asked in great concern.

"If I were you," the repairman said, "I'd make arrangements to stay some place else for about a week. We've fixed the old furnace temporarily. It'll last a few days. You can let us know what time would be convenient for us to come back."

Mrs. Bobbsey explained that she would have to consult her husband and let the repairman's office know later.

In a short time the house was fairly warm again. The children took off their extra coats and settled down to an excited discussion of where they would stay while the furnace was being repaired.

"We might go to Africa," Freddie proposed. "It would be warm there, and we could see all the wild animals!"

"That's a little far," Nan teased. "But," she added, "we could go to Florida, couldn't we, Mother?"

"That would be great," Bert agreed. "I'd like some swimming."

Mrs. Bobbsey laughed. "I'm afraid we can't go either place this time. However, I had a telegram this afternoon from your father. He'll be home Tuesday. Then we can decide what to do. Perhaps we should go to the Lakeport Hotel as soon as school closes for Christmas vacation."

"Oh!" the twins chorused. "We don't want to spend Christmas there!"

CHAPTER III

A SCHOOL PROBLEM

"CHRISTMAS can be fun any place," said Mrs. Bobbsey, "if one remembers the true spirit of the day."

"Of course," Nan murmured dreamily, then added, "Bert, come on down to the cellar. We have some secret business in the workshop."

"You bet." He grinned mysteriously.

The next morning Lakeport resembled a sparkling fairyland. Flossie, running to her bedroom window, squealed with delight. "Oh, Nan!" she cried to her still drowsy sister, with whom she shared a room. "The whole world's got vanilla frosting!"

Another feathery layer of snow softened the outlines of trees and houses, and the streets were hidden under the silent white blanket.

After breakfast the four twins hurriedly

donned their snow boots, coats, and hats, said good-by to Snap, the Bobbseys' big white dog, and Snoop, their black cat, and started for school.

"Whoopee!" Freddie yelled, running down the front steps and rolling over and over in the clean, bright snow. "I'm a polar bear!"

"Shh, Freddie!" Flossie whispered. "You tiptoe in fairyland, remember?"

"Or you get spanked if you let snowdrops soak your school suit," Nan joked as she looked at her young brother's wet clothes.

Freddie gazed about him. The quiet, clear morning did seem unreal. The stillness of the December day was not broken until the Bobbseys reached the school yard. There, pandemonium seemed to have broken loose!

The sound of shouts and running feet made the twins quicken their pace. What could have happened?

A crowd of youngsters was gathered around the wide front door of the school, but finally Bert managed to squeeze his way through. Nan, Flossie, and Freddie, also curious, followed him.

On the front steps stood an enormous snowball—so big that it completely blocked the double doors of the school entrance. The school handyman was trying to pry the frozen ball loose with a long lever.

"Who put it there?" Nan asked.

"Let me help," Bert offered, and heaved his weight against the mass of snow as the man pushed on the lever. Soon several of the older boys rushed forward to assist.

But the huge doorstop had apparently been soaked with water, freezing it solidly to the step. Five more minutes passed before the obstruction was worked loose. In the meantime the children had entered the building through a side door.

Shortly after nine, teachers informed their pupils that Mr. Tetlow, the school principal, had called a special assembly—all grades were to go to the auditorium immediately.

On their way, Bert and Nan tried to guess the reason for the meeting. "I'll bet it has something to do with that snowball blocking the front door," Bert surmised. "I have a feeling somebody's in for plenty of trouble!"

A few minutes later Mr. Tetlow, a tall, pleasant-looking man, mounted the stage and began to speak. "I presume you have guessed that this meeting has been called to determine who placed the huge snowball at the front entrance of the building. This prank might have had very serious consequences as it is against the fire laws to block any entrance to a school building. If the guilty persons will come forward now, there will be no punishment."

He paused and waited a minute. The auditorium was very still. No one moved.

"Well," Mr. Tetlow continued, "I think it only fair, students, to tell you that I have a clue that points very definitely to one of the troublemakers."

Still no one stood up. Mr. Tetlow sighed. "I am sorry the makers of the snowball do not choose to confess, but I shall be in my office all day and will be glad to see anybody who has information about this prank. Assembly dismissed!"

The children filed silently from the room, but the minute they reached the hall the chatter began. Charlie came up to Bert. "Whoever did it might as well own up," he remarked. "Mr. Tetlow says he has a good clue."

Bert agreed and they hurried off to their classes. At lunchtime it was discovered that no one had as yet confessed and there were all sorts of rumors as to the culprit.

During the last period of the day a boy came into Bert's home room with the message that Bert was wanted in the principal's office. Nan looked up, startled, as her twin arose immediately and left the room.

"What could Mr. Tetlow want me for?" Bert thought uneasily. "Does he believe I had something to do with that stunt?"

When Bert reached the school office, the secretary told him to take a seat in Mr. Tetlow's study and wait. A moment later the principal appeared, closed the study door, and sat down at his desk. His face was sad.

"Well, Bert," he began, "I've waited all day for you. I can understand why you may not have wanted to say anything at assembly, but I did hope you'd come here of your own accord. I'll give you another chance. Is there something you want to tell me about the unfortunate episode at the school door?"

Bert looked puzzled. "You—you mean about the snowball?" he asked, and at the principal's nod, added, "No, sir. I had nothing to do with it!"

"Hmmm." Mr. Tetlow rubbed his chin thoughtfully and gazed out the window. "I'm afraid I'm led to believe otherwise, Bert."

Leaning forward, he picked up an object from his desk. "This knife was found by the handyman *under* the snowball, Bert. It has the initials B. B. on the handle. Examine it, please."

Bert walked over to the desk and took the knife. He turned it over and over, then felt in all his pockets.

"Is it yours, Bert?" Mr. Tetlow asked sternly.

Without searching his pants pockets, Bert had known at once that the knife was his. He stared at it, however, with a puzzled frown.

"Does the knife belong to you?" the principal repeated as he studied Bert's face.

"Yes—yes, sir, it does," Bert replied.

An uncomfortable silence followed the admission. While he was wondering how his knife could possibly have been placed underneath the snowball, Mr. Tetlow was waiting for him to make a confession.

"If I could only remember when I last had it with me," Bert thought frantically, staring out the window which faced on the street.

"Ahem!" Mr. Tetlow cleared his throat expectantly.

Bert suddenly stood up excitedly. "Mr. Tetlow, I think I can prove that I wasn't the guilty one," he cried out.

The principal's eyebrows lifted, but he made no reply.

"That gentleman who is just passing the school—Mr. Carford," Bert continued eagerly. "Would you have someone ask him to come in here, sir? I think he may be able to prove my innocence."

Mr. Tetlow hesitated a moment, then quickly called in his secretary and asked her to do as Bert had suggested. A few minutes later, the elderly man entered the principal's office.

"Good afternoon, Tetlow," he said cordially, shaking hands with the principal and nodding to Bert. "I'm curious to know why you called me in here."

"It's nice to see you, Carford," Mr. Tetlow replied. "Bert Bobbsey here is in a little trouble, and he seems to think you can help him. He will explain."

"What's the matter, young fellow?" Mr. Carford asked, smiling.

Bert took a deep breath. "I wondered, sir, if you had found anything in your car last night after you let me out at my home?"

"Why, yes, as a matter of fact, I did," the elderly man replied. "Your knife! Remember when you stumbled getting into the car? You must have dropped it on the floor then. Evidently it slid over to my side of the car because I didn't find it until I got home. What's this all about?"

Without answering Mr. Carford's question, Mr. Tetlow picked up the knife from his desk. "Is this the one?" he asked.

Mr. Carford nodded, looking puzzled.

"What did you do with the knife after you found it, sir?" Bert asked politely.

Mr. Carford explained that he had planned to call Bert after supper and tell him of his find. "But young Jimmy Belton, who lives next door to us, stopped at our house to bring my sister a magazine and said he was going into town. I gave him the knife to leave at Bert's home."

Mr. Tetlow described the prank with the snowball and how Bert had been implicated. "Let's get to the bottom of this," he said. Buzzing his secretary again, he asked her to bring Jimmy Belton to his office immediately.

In a few minutes Jimmy walked in. The ten-year-old boy's eyes widened when he saw Bert and Mr. Carford. The principal asked him what he had done with Bert's knife after Mr. Carford had given it to him to return.

"Why, I gave it to Danny Rugg," Jimmy replied. "I met Danny near the Bobbseys' corner.

Danny asked me what I was doing there, and I told him I was going to return Bert's knife. He said he was going to see Bert anyway and would give him the knife. Didn't he do it?"

"I'm afraid not," Mr. Tetlow replied grimly. "I'm beginning to understand what happened. I'll have Danny in here now."

Bert, too, thought he knew the answer to the riddle. He remembered Danny's threat to get even for the snow fort incident!

When the bully entered the principal's office, he had a look of bravado on his face. But when he saw Bert, Jimmy, and the principal glance from him to the knife, his eyes took on an alarmed expression.

"Danny, did you put Bert's knife under that snowball?" Mr. Tetlow asked sternly.

The bully hung his head and managed to choke out, "Y—yes."

The principal's fingers drummed on his knee. "I think you owe Bert an apology," he said.

Danny stared at Bert, his eyes blazing with fury.

"We're waiting," Mr. Tetlow said quietly.

Danny finally lowered his head and mumbled, "I apologize."

"Okay, Danny," Bert said generously.

Mr. Tetlow rose from his chair. "Very well. Now, Danny, obviously you didn't place that snowball on the steps without some help. I don't expect you to carry tales, but I do think that when you tell your friends you have confessed, they will want to also. I suggest that you ask them to come to my office immediately."

Mr. Tetlow shook hands with Mr. Carford, thanking him for his help. The elderly man put an arm about Bert's shoulder and they left the room together.

"Thanks a lot for clearing me," Bert said as he escorted his friend to the door of the building.

Mr. Carford shook hands with the boy as he left. "I'm always glad to do a favor for a Bobbsey. Remember, you stopped Daisy for me! Besides, I—"

Bert waited hopefully to hear more.

CHAPTER IV

THE DOG SLEIGH

LOOKING sad and mysterious again, Mr. Carford stopped speaking and walked off.

Bert shook his head as he watched the man's retreating figure. "I can't make him out," he mused. "He acts so nice and friendly, then all at once he seems to close up." Still puzzled by Mr. Carford's strange behavior, Bert returned to his classroom.

When school was over, he and Charlie Mason walked out together. As they passed the principal's office, Charlie pointed to a group of boys filing into the room. "They're the same ones who were in Danny's gang yesterday at the snow fort," he said.

"Every one of them," Bert agreed. "I'm glad they're owning up."

Charlie chuckled. "It must have been a lot of work, making that snowball," he said. "And just

to get even with you! I'm afraid Danny'll be a
long time getting over this, Bert. Better be on
the lookout for more mean tricks."

Nan caught up to Bert a couple of blocks
from home and listened eagerly to his account of
the scene in the school office.

"When I thanked Mr. Carford for coming to
my rescue," Bert concluded, "he said he was always glad to do a favor for a Bobbsey. But the
strange thing was that he looked so odd when he
said it."

"That is queer," Nan agreed. "I can't wait for
Dad to come home so we can learn what this
Snow Lodge mystery really is all about. Maybe
there's some way we can help Mr. Carford."

Meanwhile Freddie and Flossie, already
home from school, were playing in the snow in
front of their house. "I know what!" the little
girl exclaimed. "Let's make our own sleigh. We
can tie a box on your sled, Freddie—"

"And Snap can be the horse!" her twin interrupted. "What'll we use for harness and reins?"

Flossie's brow furrowed. "Well," she said
thoughtfully, "we can use Snap's leash for the
harness, and—I know! My long hair ribbons
will make pretty reins."

"Swell!" her brother replied. "You get your
ribbons and I'll find the sled and the box and
the leash." He started toward the house, calling,
"Snap! Here, boy!"

Around a corner of the house bounded the dog, who had once belonged to a circus. Seeing his young master and mistress, Snap barked joyously and walked toward them on his hind feet along a shoveled path. Freddie patted him lovingly while Flossie hurried inside the house.

Fifteen minutes later, everything was ready for the sleigh trip. Freddie had torn the top and front side from a large paper packing box and tied it onto his sled. Flossie helped her twin make the final adjustments on the harness. At last Freddie straightened and said:

"That should do it. Did you tie those ribbons together real tight?" At Flossie's nod, he added, "Well, climb aboard!"

Freddie sat in the back of the box with Flossie in front. Each child took one of the ribbon reins. "Giddap!" they cried together, and Snap, with one questioning glance back at his drivers, started off, giving an excited bark.

"It works!" Flossie cried triumphantly as the homemade sleigh skimmed over the snow.

Eyes dancing and cheeks a bright pink from the wind, both twins yelled, "Faster! Faster!" to the obliging Snap.

"Those ribbons had better hold!" Freddie yelled as Snap hesitated, turned in a wide arc, and dashed pell-mell up a side street.

"Hey!" the little boy cried. "I thought *we* were driving this sleigh! Where's Snap going?"

Flossie, breathless from their sudden speed, pointed ahead and gasped, "Nan and Bert!"

Some distance up the street the older twins stood staring in surprise at the dog and sled racing toward them.

"It's Snap!" Bert exclaimed. "Whoa, boy! Slow down!" he called. "Pull back on the reins, Freddie and Flossie!"

The younger children obeyed, and Snap's pace slowed to a walk. But when he reached Bert and Nan, the dog leaped up and put his paws on the boy's shoulders.

As the animal rose, so did the front of the sled! The reins broke, and Freddie and Flossie tumbled out head over heels!

Laughing and sputtering from the snow in their faces, the young twins scrambled to their feet and righted the sleigh.

"Don't you know that's not the way to pull a sleigh?" Flossie said, pretending to scold Snap, who stood looking up at her, his tail wagging furiously.

"Poor Snap is tired out," Nan said, smiling as she leaned down to pat the dog. "Why don't you two come on home with us and let him rest?"

Obligingly, Freddie and Flossie removed the reins from the dog's collar. Then, pulling the sled, both fell into step with Bert and Nan.

"What happened about the frozen snowball on the school steps?" Freddie asked eagerly.

Bert gave him a full account of the scene in the principal's office. Freddie clenched his fists. "I'd like to get even with Danny Rugg!" he cried.

Flossie also looked indignant. "It was mean of Mr. Tetlow to think you did it, Bert!"

"Well, my knife was found under the snowball so I can't blame him for believing I had something to do with it. And he did give me a chance to clear myself." Bert defended the principal.

"That's right," Nan agreed. "Wasn't it lucky that Mr. Carford came by just at that moment?"

"I like Mr. Carford," Freddie said. "He's a real Santa Claus."

By this time the children had reached the Bobbsey house. Their mother met them at the door, and again Bert had to tell about the huge snowball and Mr. Carford's help.

Mrs. Bobbsey put one arm around Bert. "Well," she said, "I'm glad everything turned out all right. Danny is certainly a mischief maker."

"Why are you wearing your heavy sweater, Mommy?" Flossie asked. "Are you going out?"

Mrs. Bobbsey frowned. "No, dear, but the furnace isn't giving us much heat. Dinah is staying near the oven in the kitchen, and I had to put on this sweater."

"Ooh, it *is* cold!" Nan exclaimed, shivering as she removed her heavy coat.

"I think you'd all better put on sweaters," their mother said. "I don't want you taking cold —especially just before Christmas."

"What are we going to do about Christmas, Mother?" Nan asked eagerly.

Mrs. Bobbsey gave an anxious sigh. "I don't know! I've called all the hotels in town and they're booked solid for the holidays. The only thing they can do is to call us if there are any cancellations."

"I guess we're out of luck," Bert said sadly.

"Your father will be home tomorrow," Mrs. Bobbsey reminded the twins. "I'm sure he'll know what to do."

"I'll be so glad to see Daddy," Flossie said. "It seems as if he'd been away for years and years!"

"I have an idea about what we can do now to get warmer," Nan spoke up.

"What?" they all chorused.

"Let's play hide and seek. I'll be 'it.' "

They all looked at Mrs. Bobbsey. "May we, Mommy?" Flossie asked, her eyes dancing in anticipation.

"Yes, if you don't upset things too much," their mother agreed. Then, relieved that the children were in better spirits, she settled down on the sofa with some mending.

Nan hid her eyes in her arm and began to count slowly. The other three children tiptoed carefully from the room.

"Ninety-nine, one hundred!" Nan cried. "Here I come, ready or not!"

She ran out into the hall and flung open the door of the coat closet. No one was there. Then as she started into the dining room, Flossie raced down the stairs and into the living room, crying, "Home free!"

Now Nan began to climb the stairs. There was a giggle and Freddie ran from behind the tall clock in the lower hall. "I'm free, too!" he called, as he gained the living-room sofa.

Laughing, Nan went on up the stairs, and a few minutes later Freddie and Flossie heard her cry, "I see you, Bert!" as the boy emerged from the clothes closet in Nan and Flossie's bedroom.

When the children had gathered in the living room again, panting from their game, Mrs.

Bobbsey looked up. "I was so worried about the furnace," she explained, "that I forgot to tell you something, Bert and Nan. You have letters on the mantel."

"Hooray!" Bert exclaimed. "I hope mine's from Harry. He hasn't written to me for a long time!" Harry was the son of the children's Uncle Daniel Bobbsey. The Lakeport Bobbseys had had many good times at their cousin Harry's home, Meadowbrook Farm.

"Maybe mine's from Dorothy Minturn!" Nan said eagerly. Cousin Dorothy lived at Ocean Cliff. Her mother was Mrs. Bobbsey's sister, and the young cousins were all good friends.

In another minute the older twins had opened their letters, and each was busily reading. Bert spoke first. "Listen to this, from Harry:

"Just between you and me, Bert, I'm going to have a terrible Christmas. Mother and Dad and I are going to visit old Aunt Martha for the holidays. She must be at least a hundred, and there aren't any boys around to play with. I'll be glad when we get home again!"

Mrs. Bobbsey looked sympathetic. "Poor Harry!" she said. "I agree it won't be much fun for him."

Nan looked up from her letter. "Dorothy is having the same trouble," she announced. "Uncle William and Aunt Emily are taking her to Florida for the holidays. Dorothy says she has lots of swimming in the summer and wants to spend the Christmas holidays where there's snow. But there doesn't seem to be any hope of that!"

"It looks," Bert observed wryly, "as if all the Bobbsey children are in the same boat. No place to spend Christmas that we like!"

"Wouldn't it be great," Nan said, "if we could all be together some place?" The other twins nodded and grinned.

"It would be a cousin Christmas," Flossie observed.

CHAPTER V

PART OF THE SECRET

THE NEXT day at school was spent by the twins and many of their friends in putting on a Christmas play. Flossie was an adorable angel, Freddie the innkeeper. Bert was a shepherd, while Nan played the part of Mary.

Danny and his pals seemed very subdued and went out of their way to avoid Bert. Because the bully had been responsible for blocking the school entrance with the huge snowball, there was a good deal of teasing about snowballs.

As the twins met after school, Nan said, "Let's go past the lumberyard office and see if Dad's back." To their delight, he was.

"Oh, Daddy!" Flossie cried, rushing up and throwing her arms about her tall, handsome father. "We're so glad you're home!"

"Yes, we have lots to tell you!" Freddie announced.

Everyone talked at once. It was several minutes before Bert had a chance to ask Mr. Bobbsey about the mysterious Mr. Carford.

"What did he mean about a Bobbsey coming into his life five years ago, Dad?"

The twins' father looked grave for a moment, then said, "Well, Bert—" He was interrupted by the telephone. After listening a few moments, he said, "Will you hold the line, please?"

Turning to the twins, Mr. Bobbsey told them this was an important, long-distance call. "You run along now. I'll see you all at supper."

The children waved good-by and filed out. Halfway home they suddenly heard the tinkle of bells behind them. Turning, they saw Mr. Carford's beautiful old sleigh coming along the street.

The old man stopped his horse as he drew abreast of the Bobbseys and called a hearty "Hi there!"

When they had returned the greetings, he asked, "Would you children like to have a sleigh ride out to my home? I know my sister baked some cookies this morning, and—" he grinned, "there's a surprise there I know you'll enjoy."

"Oh, we'd love to come!" chorused Flossie and Freddie. Nan and Bert also accepted the invitation.

Mr. Carford drove by the Bobbsey home, and the twins' mother gladly gave permission for the visit.

The older twins climbed into the rear seat of the sleigh, while the young ones took seats on either side of Mr. Carford. Then they were off.

"Whoopee! This is great!" shouted Freddie a few minutes later, as Mr. Carford gave him the reins to hold. Freddie guided the horse importantly along the snowy road.

Shortly they drew up in front of an old farmhouse nestled among majestic pines, which swayed gently in the wind. A wisp of smoke curled from a huge stone chimney atop the shingled roof.

As the children scrambled to the ground, a plump woman came and stood in the front door and called a cheery welcome.

"This is my sister, Miss Emma Carford," said their host. The maiden lady had gray hair and blue eyes much like Mr. Carford's.

Miss Carford led the children inside the homey dwelling. While they removed their coats and Mr. Carford put Daisy in the stall, she brought out a snack of sugar cookies and milk.

"Yummy!" exclaimed Flossie. "These cookies are wonderful!"

"You're a good cook!" burst out Freddie, who considered himself an expert on such matters. The others laughed.

When the Bobbseys had finished, the Carfords took them on a tour of inspection of the house. Nan was interested in the old-time four-poster beds on the second floor, for they were topped by canopies and covered with bright-colored patchwork quilts made by Miss Carford.

Her brother showed Bert his collection of Toby mugs which he had obtained on trips to England. Many of the little containers, which were shaped like jolly figures, dated back before the Revolutionary War.

Finally the group ended up in the kitchen, where there was a wide fireplace with a raised hearth such as those used in olden days. Bert helped Mr. Carford build a fire, and soon the flames gave the room a cheerful warmth.

"What are you children planning to do in your Christmas vacation?" Miss Carford asked.

"We're probably going to have a hotel Christmas!" Freddie replied mournfully.

"A what?" the white-haired lady asked, and Nan and Bert told her about the furnace repairs.

"I like hotels," Flossie confided, "but not at Christmastime. We couldn't have a big Christmas tree in a little bedroom—"

The Carfords looked at each other but made no comment. In a few moments the elderly man said, "I copied this fireplace from one in Snow Lodge. How my brothers and sisters and I loved to sit in front of that one when we were children! It was a wonderful way to spend a long winter evening after a hard day's work on the farm."

Snow Lodge! Bert and Nan exchanged excited

glances as Mr. Carford paused. Perhaps now they would learn something about the mystery after all!

"Our parents died when we children were small," Mr. Carford continued. "Snow Lodge had to be sold, and each of us went to live with a different older relative. Over the years all except Emma and me were married. Gradually we lost touch with one another."

The man's blue eyes stared reminiscently into the fire. Finally he went on to say that when he had grown up he went to New York, where he had prospered in business. Finally he had retired, however, and decided to return to Lakeport. He had bought back Snow Lodge.

"I was lonely," he confessed, "and hoped that some members of my family might like to live with me at the lodge. But they all had their own homes and did not want to."

"That was too bad," Nan said sympathetically.

Mr. Carford patted the girl on her shoulder and said, "Don't feel sorry for me, because I've had a happy life for the most part. Besides, modernizing Snow Lodge kept me busy for some time. After the remodeling was done, I—"

"Oh, there they are!" Miss Carford interrupted. Glancing at her wrist watch, she added, "Right on time, too."

She pointed out the wide kitchen window and

the children saw an unusual sight—at least ten deer.

"Is this the surprise you told us about?" Freddie asked Mr. Carford, as they all donned coats and hats to go outside.

The white-haired gentleman nodded and smiled. "Yes. They come from the woods beyond my farm. We've trained them to eat from our hands." He asked Bert to get a sack of grain from the pantry and to bring some lettuce from the refrigerator.

Eagerly, the Bobbseys tiptoed out the back door and quietly approached the beautiful, shy animals. Their large brown eyes darted about nervously until the children held out handfuls of grain and lettuce. Then, timidly, the deer edged closer.

A young fawn softly nuzzled Flossie's palm.

"Oh, mine's adorable!" exclaimed the little girl. "Please, may I take him home with me?" Without waiting for an answer, Flossie went on, "And I'll call you Softy, 'cause that's what you are." She flung her arms around the startled animal's neck and hugged him.

Nan smiled and went to Flossie's side. "I'm afraid Softy would be terribly lonesome at our house, honey," she said kindly.

"But—but he'd have me!" Flossie insisted. Then she paused. "You're right, Nan. Softy might run away and get lost."

Flossie turned back to her fawn. She gave the animal another quick hug, then whispered, "Good-by, Softy. Be a good deer and don't get hurt."

The older twins winked at the Carfords. A few minutes later the deer, their hunger satis-

fied, bounded back into the forest. Everyone returned to the kitchen, and Mr. Carford resumed his story.

"As I started to say, children, after the remodeling was done at Snow Lodge, I received word that my elder sister, Louise Burdock, had

been widowed. She was left with a ten-year-old boy, Dave, and had very little money. I invited them to come to Snow Lodge and live with me. They accepted. Not long after they arrived in Lakeport, however, Louise died. So I brought up Dave alone."

"How wonderful of you!" Nan murmured.

"Dave was a fine boy," said Mr. Carford. "He became like a son to me. We had grand times studying together, taking hikes in the woods, fishing, hunting, and—"

Suddenly a sad expression flickered briefly on the man's face as he added, "But then, about five years ago, there was a—a misunderstanding between us. Dave left Snow Lodge. He will not return, unless—"

Nan and Bert looked at each other. Could this be the mystery they were curious about?

Regaining his composure, Mr. Carford concluded, "So I closed Snow Lodge and hired a neighboring farmer to keep it in good shape. When Emma," he glanced at his sister, "wrote that she would like to stay with me, I bought this farmhouse."

He stopped speaking, and there was a long silence. Bert decided that the "misunderstanding" between Mr. Carford and his nephew must have been very serious.

"Apparently Mr. Carford isn't going to tell us what it is," thought Nan in disappointment.

She looked at the kitchen clock. It was four-thirty. "We must be getting home," she said.

"You'll forgive an old man for talking so long," Mr. Carford apologized, as his sister went for the twins' coats, hats, and boots. "But I've enjoyed your visit. Will you come again some time?"

"We sure will," said Freddie stoutly.

As the twins prepared to leave, there was a sudden uproar in the back yard. Chickens squawked frantically. A dog howled. What was going on?

CHAPTER VI

A BAD SPILL

FOR A moment, the group in the Carfords' kitchen was too bewildered by the sudden clamor to speak. Then, flinging open the door, Bert dashed outside.

Bounding down the back steps, he stopped short as a rock sailed past his head and landed in the chicken run. Bert spun about just in time to catch a glimpse of the thrower running away.

"Wonder who he is," Bert thought, as he noted a stocky figure hiding under a black cape held loosely over a dark blue ski cap and jacket. The person ran across the field and disappeared in the woods beyond.

Meanwhile, Nan, the small twins, and the Carfords had hurried out to join Bert. "That could be Danny," Freddie suggested.

"But what would Danny be doing out here?" Nan asked, puzzled.

"And why should he throw rocks at my chickens?" Mr. Carford demanded.

Thoughtfully Bert said, "Remember the pocketknife business? You helped clear me, Mr. Carford. I showed Danny up, and he probably holds a grudge against us both. That is—if it *was* Danny!"

"I'd say the stone-thrower, whoever he is, needs a good spanking!" Miss Carford exclaimed tartly, and her brother agreed.

"I'm going after him!" Bert exclaimed, and Nan, Flossie, and Freddie cried in unison, "Me too!"

With the older boy in the lead, the twins dashed across the field and entered the woods. The culprit was out of sight, but had left a fresh trail of footprints in the snow.

"We'd better hurry, or he'll get away!" Bert urged.

The twins ran as fast as they dared, slipping and sliding in the snow. Presently the boy's footprints they were following merged with those of men. The trek continued, however. Gradually one set of the larger footprints after another led off to narrow side paths. But the smaller tracks went on through the woods.

"Now we policemen are getting somewhere," Freddie said manfully.

He had just finished speaking when Bert, who was still in the lead, stopped suddenly. "The tracks end here," he announced. "And the snow is all packed down as if someone had sat down."

Nan pointed ahead. "Weren't those thin lines made by ice-skate runners?" she asked.

"Of course!" said Bert. "Good for you, Nan! This is a frozen stream which runs into Lake Metoka. It's covered with snow. Whoever threw those rocks must have skated away from here. Let's follow the marks!"

The twins went on. In a few minutes the stream widened. Suddenly Bert stiffened. He pointed across the frozen water to a point near the far bank.

A boy dressed in a blue ski cap and jacket was skating slowly in a circle!

"That's Danny!" all four children exclaimed.

As they watched, the boy hurled a large stone at something on the bank. There was a flurry of snow and a squirrel scampered away.

"The meanie!" Flossie cried out.

"That and his clothes are pretty good proof Danny threw the rocks at Mr. Carford's chickens," Bert declared. "I'm going over and see."

"We'll go with you," the others responded.

The twins started off across the snow-covered stream. When they were about fifty yards from the boy, Bert yelled, "Hey, Danny!"

Startled, Danny spun about, almost falling on the ice as he did so. His face clouded with anger at sight of the Bobbseys.

"What are you kids doing way out here?" Danny sneered. "Aren't you scared of getting lost?"

"We're looking for someone wearing a blue ski cap and jacket who was at Mr. Carford's farm," Bert replied. "He was throwing rocks at the chickens."

Freddie put in, "Danny, what did you do with your black cape?"

Danny looked indignant. "I don't know what you're talking about!" he blustered.

"I'll explain," Bert said quietly. "We followed the tracks of the rock-thrower. They led us right here to you!"

"You think you're such smart detectives, don't you?" Danny yelled. "Well, this time you're wrong! I wasn't near any farm, and I don't own any black cape!"

With that he lashed out at Bert, hitting him squarely on the chin. More surprised than hurt, Bert staggered back off balance. His foot slipped and he fell, sliding on his back across the ice.

Nan's eyes grew wide with alarm. Her twin was sliding head first toward a ragged tree stump on the bank!

"Look out!" Nan cried, lunging toward Bert in an attempt to save him from a bad injury.

Before she could help, Freddie was tripped by Danny and the little boy sprawled full length in front of her, face downward.

Nan's warning, however, had alerted Bert to his danger. With all the strength he could muster, Bert dug his right heel into the snow-covered ice, then pushed hard with his right hand. The two actions turned the direction of his slide, and he avoided the stump!

At last he stopped sliding. Bert scrambled to his feet and hurried to the side of Freddie, who had had the wind knocked out of him.

"Freddie, are you okay?"

"I—I guess so," the little boy answered. "But give Danny a punch for me."

"Yes," said Flossie. "He's the worst boy in Lakeport."

But doing this proved to be impossible. Danny was skimming rapidly down the stream. The Bobbseys would never be able to catch him without skates!

Bert shook his head in disgust. "I sure muffed it letting Danny get away! But I'll corner him tomorrow," he promised himself, "and find out the truth!"

The four children returned to the farmhouse and a few minutes later were homeward bound in Mr. Carford's car. When they reached the Bobbsey house, Nan invited him to come in.

The old man smiled. "As a matter of fact, if you hadn't, I was going to invite myself in."

The twins' father greeted the caller cordially, took his coat, then introduced him to Mrs. Bobbsey.

"I hear you're having furnace trouble," Mr. Carford remarked, "and are talking of going to a hotel for the holidays."

"That's right," Mr. Bobbsey replied.

Suddenly Mr. Carford drew a key case from his pocket. "These belong to Snow Lodge," he said. "I would be very happy if you and your family would spend the holidays at the lodge."

"Why, how very kind of you!" Mrs. Bobbsey exclaimed, and the twins gave whoops of joy.

"Not at all," Mr. Carford smiled. "I don't know anyone who would enjoy the place more, unless—"

The old gentleman did not finish his sentence and Nan noted that her father darted a sympathetic glance toward Mr. Carford.

"At any rate," their guest continued briskly, "the place is yours for as long as you wish to use it. What do you say?"

Mr. Bobbsey grinned. "We accept!" He took the keys. "You don't know how I appreciate your offer. The children can have a real old-fashioned Christmas."

"What do you mean, Daddy?" Flossie spoke up.

"I'll explain later, little fat fairy," her father said, using his pet name for her.

Mr. Carford's blue eyes twinkled as he turned to the children. "I'm sure you'd find plenty to do up there—ice skating, skiing, sledding. And if you have to stay indoors, there are several trunks in the attic that should provide good dress-up costumes. And then there are all sorts of secret closets in the place."

"Oh boy, that's for me!" Bert said excitedly.

Freddie and Flossie dashed across the room and threw their arms around the tall old man.

Nan turned to her father and pleaded, "Dad, please let's go Thursday. Then we can get ready for our Christmas in the woods!"

"You're welcome to go up there any time," Mr. Carford said. "Well, I must be getting back or Emma's supper will be ruined." Then he added, "Suppose I pick you younger twins up after school tomorrow. We'll play Santa Claus."

Flossie spoke up. "We get out early—noon-time."

"All the better. I'll come for you here at the house directly after lunch," Mr. Carford said.

Everyone crowded about the elderly man as Mr. Bobbsey helped him on with his coat.

Nan looked up at him. "Mr. Carford, if Mother and Dad will let us, would you mind ter-ribly if we brought two more children?"

"Of course not," the owner of Snow Lodge said. "The more the merrier. Did you have a couple of playmates in mind?"

"No. Our cousins," Nan replied, and told Mr. Carford about the letters she and Bert had re-ceived.

"Have them, by all means," the kindly old gentleman said.

Nan turned to her mother and father. "May we invite Harry and Dorothy to spend the holi-days with us while their parents are away?"

Mr. and Mrs. Bobbsey exchanged glances and nodded. "Go ahead," said Mrs. Bobbsey. "You know, I'm beginning to be really excited about this trip myself. Let's try to start Thursday."

"All right," her husband agreed.

Nan flew to the telephone and put in first one call, then the other. There was no answer, and finally she received a report that bad storms had affected the systems and the lines were out of order.

"Oh dear!" said Nan. "What'll I do? There isn't time to send a letter."

"Let's telegraph," Bert proposed. "Then Harry and Dorothy can call us when the phones are working again."

The twins sat down to compose the messages, and Nan sent them. It was not until the family was seated at the table that Bert finally found an opportunity to ask his father about the mystery of Snow Lodge.

"Dad, did you do him a favor in the past?" he said.

"Yes," Mr. Bobbsey replied slowly. "It's not a very happy tale. Mr. Carford brought up his nephew, Dave Burdock, after the lad's mother died. He gave the boy many things and, I'm afraid, spoiled him to the extent that Dave had little regard for money."

"What did he do?" asked Flossie, wide-eyed.

"Dave liked to spend freely," Mr. Bobbsey continued, "and though his uncle gave him a generous allowance, Dave frequently asked for more. One day, when he was eighteen years old, he asked Mr. Carford for a large sum and his uncle refused him—for the very first time.

"The two had an argument. Later in the day Mr. Carford missed a stack of bills he had left on a mantelpiece, intending to bank the money on his trip into town that day. Since Dave and Mr. Carford were the only ones at home, Mr. Carford accused the boy of taking the money."

"Did he?" Freddie asked.

"Dave said he was innocent," his father replied. "But his uncle didn't believe him. They had a violent quarrel and Dave, deeply hurt by the accusation, left Snow Lodge. He vowed never to return or to see his uncle again until his name was cleared."

"What a pity!" Mrs. Bobbsey sighed. "But you helped him, Dick, didn't you?"

"Yes," her husband said.

Mr. Bobbsey added that he had known Dave and believed that he was innocent.

"I found him a room in town and gave him a job at the lumberyard until he could decide what he wanted to do. This was five years ago, when Nan and Bert were young children and Freddie and Flossie were babies."

"What does Dave do now?" Bert asked.

"Dave loves the outdoors, so he works as a guide for winter sportsmen in the woods not far from Snow Lodge. He lives in a cozy cabin near there. In the summer, Dave goes to the North Woods as a fishermen's guide. But he has never forgiven his uncle for accusing him of the theft."

"What about the money?" Nan asked.

"That's still a mystery," Mr. Bobbsey replied.

"Thinking that a prowler might have broken in, the police made a thorough search of Snow Lodge. But there was no sign of any intruder. They finally decided that the money might have fallen into the fireplace, where a blaze was burning, and been destroyed."

"Poor Mr. Carford—and poor Dave," said Nan. "No wonder Mr. Carford looks sad sometimes. I'll bet he misses his nephew."

Mr. Bobbsey nodded. "Yes, he's heartsick about the whole affair. You know, Dave is his heir, along with Mr. Carford's sister Emma. I think the old gentleman would like to forget the incident, but Dave is very proud—"

The twins were silent for a moment, thinking about the puzzle. Mr. Bobbsey left the room, saying he wanted to make a telephone call.

"If we go to Snow Lodge, let's search for the money," Freddie suggested.

"Sure," Bert agreed. "It might still be there somewhere."

CHAPTER VII

THREE SANTAS

THE next day school was adjourned at noon, marking the beginning of the Christmas vacation. The Bobbseys hurried home and learned that lunch would be a little late. Dinah had spent most of the morning helping the twins' mother pack and bake holiday cookies to be taken to Snow Lodge.

"Isn't it 'citing?" Flossie said.

At this instant the telephone rang, and Nan rushed to answer it. "Dorothy!" she shrieked. "You got my telegram?"

"Sure. It was delivered yesterday. The phone lines have just been fixed."

"Can you come?" Nan asked. "Oh, I hope—"

"Guess what!" Dorothy cried out. "I'm packed and ready to take the train! Can you meet me?"

"*Can* we?" Nan almost shouted.

"My train reaches Lakeport at five."

"We'll be there."

"Good-by now. I have to run."

A few minutes later Harry called Bert. "What time is supper at your house tonight?" he asked.

"You're coming!" Bert yelled.

"You bet. I'll be down on the bus. Be at your house by six."

"That's keen!" said Bert. "And Harry, there's a mystery connected with Snow Lodge."

"What! Oh boy, will we have fun solving it!" said Harry, then hung up.

While waiting for lunch, Flossie and Freddie huddled together on the sofa in the living room over a sheet of paper. They began to write out a list of everything they wanted to take with them to Snow Lodge.

"Flossie, how do you spell *engine?*" asked her twin.

"Like in fire engine?" Flossie teased, knowing very well that Freddie meant his toy fire-fighting apparatus.

"Naturally," Freddie answered. "I have to take my hook and ladder set along."

Flossie nodded seriously, for many times her brother had helped to put out little fires with his equipment. "But I'm not sure how it's spelled," she said dubiously.

Her twin shrugged. "Never mind, you can bet I won't forget that toy."

The little boy put down his pencil and jumped up. "I'd better test the engine now to make sure everything's working right. We might have to use it at Snow Lodge some time."

"Good idea, Freddie," Flossie said approvingly. "I'll come and watch you."

In a few minutes Freddie had filled the pump of his truck with water and started to race from room to room, putting out imaginary fires. While Flossie watched, he squirted the fireplace and a large plant on a living-room table.

"It works perfectly," he said with satisfaction.

Just then there was a sharp cry from the kitchen.

"That sounded like Dinah!" Flossie exclaimed, and the twins raced to the kitchen.

For a moment they could see nothing but a cloud of thick gray smoke billowing toward them. Flossie ran shouting for her mother, who was upstairs. With his eyes smarting, Freddie entered the room. In alarm, he saw that flames were shooting from the broiler in the range. Some grease must have caught on fire! But where was Dinah?

Dashing back for his fire engine, Freddie returned to the kitchen. He was about to pump water on the fire when a voice cried out:

"Stop!" It was Dinah, who came hurrying from the pantry with a box in her hand. "Don't use water on a grease fire, honey child. Use salt!"

The startled boy looked doubtful, but he grabbed the salt box from Dinah's hand and poured the white crystals freely over the flaming grease.

As the fire sputtered and was finally extinguished, Flossie and Mrs. Bobbsey rushed into the kitchen.

"Freddie put the fire out," said Dinah, and told what he had done. "He's a real live fireman!"

"With your help," Freddie said modestly. "Gee," he added, "a real, honest-to-goodness fire, and wouldn't you know I couldn't try my pumper!"

Dinah, Flossie, and Mrs. Bobbsey laughed. "But from now on you'll know exactly what to use on a grease fire," Mrs. Bobbsey pointed out. "A good fireman should know about all types of extinguishers."

Lunch was finally served and the twins ate hungrily. They had just finished when they heard the front door chimes ring. "I'll see who's there," Flossie offered, skipping into the hall. "It's probably Mr. Santa Claus Carford."

It was the elderly man, ready to take them.

"Jingle-jangle!" cried Freddie, and raced to the door to greet Mr. Carford. "I'll be ready in a flash!"

Mr. Carford chuckled and shook hands with Mrs. Bobbsey, who had followed the twins.

While she talked with their new friend, Freddie and Flossie dashed upstairs for extra sweaters and warm coats. On the way down, Flossie noticed that her twin was stuffing a toy hook and ladder inside his coat.

"What's that for?" she asked.

Freddie blushed. "Well, I just thought maybe Mr. Carford wouldn't have enough toys to go around for all the children on his list, and—say, what do you have there?"

He pointed to a pretty little doll with red hair that Flossie was tucking into the big pocket of her coat.

"I guess I had the same idea, Freddie." Flossie grinned. "Let's not tell anyone, though."

"I promise."

As the children were scrambling into the sleigh with Mr. Carford, they noticed that the whole back seat was piled high with baskets and packages. Maybe their toys would not be needed after all!

On the way to the first house, Mr. Carford said he was delighted that the Bobbseys would spend the holidays at Snow Lodge. "Your mother says it's all arranged for you to go to-morrow."

"That's right," Freddie answered, "and we're going to look and look—"

A sharp nudge in the ribs by Flossie made him catch his breath. It was his twin's way of warning him not to mention their plan to search for the missing money. Though they probably would not find it, bringing the subject up would remind Mr. Carford of his nephew.

"You're going to look—?" the man prompted.

"Oh, yes!" Freddie managed to say. "All around your wonderful house. We can't wait!"

Flossie winked at her twin. He had managed to change the subject very neatly.

After Mr. Carford left a large box of toys at a rather shabby house on the far side of town, he got back into the sleigh with a thoughtful expression.

"Do you feel sick?" Flossie asked him anxiously, as the horse trotted briskly down the snowy street.

"Of course not." Mr. Carford laughed. "I was just thinking of how much that home reminds me of the one I lived in with my aunt and uncle after my parents died. They were very poor and did not have many comforts. But they gave me kindness and a lot of love."

"Tell us about when you were little," Flossie urged, sliding her hand into Mr. Carford's large, warm one. At the moment he was holding the reins with only his left hand.

"There's not much to tell," replied their friend. "But one thing I do remember—at Christmastime there was seldom any money for presents. One time, when I was ten, I so wanted a kite to fly. I had been looking at a beautiful red-and-yellow one in a certain toy store window. How I wished my uncle would get it for me that Christmas! But I never told him. I knew it was no use."

Flossie and Freddie looked very sad after hearing this story. Poor Mr. Carford!

"Is that why you give so many toys away at this time of year?" asked Flossie.

"Yes," was the simple reply.

Freddie thought to himself that it made the generous man happy to help those children whose parents were having difficult times.

Suddenly Mr. Carford chuckled. "Well, on to our next stop, children. Giddap, Daisy!" he called to the horse. "Time's a-wastin'!"

At each of the homes Mr. Carford visited, he managed to see the children's parents, and ask them to save the gifts for Christmas morning. Finally the back of the sleigh was empty.

"Well, that's all, youngsters," he told the Bobbseys. "I'll have you home in a jiffy."

Flossie and Freddie nodded, and each felt the toy he had hidden. The twins were wondering if there were not some other child to whom they might present a little gift.

Unaware of this, Mr. Carford started to sing, "Jolly Old St. Nicholas." The sleighbells jingled, and the twins' spirits lifted as they joined in the chorus.

Suddenly Flossie cried, "Oh, look!"

Ahead of them a small boy with his face buried in his hands was seated on the curb. His little shoulders shook, and his whole body shivered.

"Why, he's crying," Freddie exclaimed. "Please stop the sleigh, Mr. Carford. Maybe we can help."

As the horse slowed, Freddie and Flossie jumped to the ground and ran over to the little fellow. They tapped him on the shoulder, but he did not look up.

"What's the matter?" Flossie asked gently.

"Are you lost?" Freddie said, and this time the short brown hair tossed in a definite no.

"C'mon," Flossie urged, putting a chubby arm around his shoulders. "Please stop crying, please do!"

The boy looked up, and the twins saw that he was about four years old. His freckled face looked woebegone, stained with tears and smudged with dirt.

"Hello," he said, then looked down at the street.

"Where do you live?" Freddie asked.

A muffled reply of, "Two-six-Pine-Street" was heard.

"That's on the way to our house," said Flossie. "We'll walk home with you. Okay?"

This time a very faint nod rewarded the twins. Returning to the sleigh, they told Mr.

Carford of their plan and thanked him for a lovely afternoon. The man smiled, said good-by, and drove off.

"Now," Freddie said brusquely to the boy, "you're too old to cry."

The gruff words seemed to work. The child brushed away his tears. Shyly he told the Bobbseys his name was Bobby Forsten.

"I don't always cry," he said defiantly.

"Neither do I," Flossie said, but with a twinkle in her eyes. "And I'm afraid to this time of year. Think how slippery our tears would make the sidewalks if they froze!"

Bobby laughed, and they started off. Three blocks down they reached the little boy's home, which turned out to be a two-family dwelling.

The twins walked up the front steps and started to push the doorbell. Suddenly Bobby sobbed, pushed open the door, and disappeared inside.

"What—" Flossie began, but Freddie waved her to silence.

Through the open door they noticed a young woman talking at a telephone booth in the hall. Her back was turned to the twins, and evidently she had not heard them or Bobby, for she was saying:

"Yes, I'm afraid Bobby and Karen know already that Santa Claus won't be leaving any presents here this year. I tried to make them understand and I think Bobby does. What can I do with my husband so ill for such a long time? It's all we can manage just to keep the house going and feed everyone. But I feel dreadful about it—"

The Bobbseys did not wait to hear more. No wonder Bobby had been crying! Here was their chance to help someone!

A moment later, when Flossie and Freddie skipped down the front steps, a small hook and ladder and a sweet-faced doll had been left behind, placed side by side in the front hall of Bobby's home.

"Merry Christmas, Karen! Merry Christmas, Bobby!" Flossie whispered softly to herself.

CHAPTER VIII

A RACE ON SKATES

WHILE Freddie and Flossie were helping Mr. Carford deliver his presents, Nan and Bert were enjoying the good skating on Lake Metoka. Every once in a while Nan would glance at her wrist watch. She must leave by four-thirty to get to the train in time to meet Dorothy.

Many of Nan and Bert's friends had heard the exciting news about the Bobbseys' vacation at Snow Lodge.

"You're sure lucky," Charlie Mason said wistfully. "Wish I could go with you."

"Oh, so do I," Nellie Parks chimed in. "You'll have lots of fun, I know."

But Grace Lavine, another friend of Nan's, was not so sure. "I've heard there's something queer about that place," she said dubiously. "I'd be afraid to stay there."

Several of the other children agreed with her

and advised the Bobbseys to be very careful when they went to the house in the woods.

"If there were anything strange about Snow Lodge, Mr. Carford would never offer to let us live in it," Nan insisted. "He's a very nice man."

Charlie put in loyally, "If there is some mystery connected with the place, I know the Bobbseys will solve it. They're good detectives."

The discussion was interrupted when one of the older boys skated up and announced that races were being planned. "They're setting up one for girls your age, Nan," he said. "Want to join in?"

Nan was eager to try her skill so she, Nellie, and Grace hurried over to the spot where the race was to begin. Charlie Mason was the starter. He held high a small branch with a red scarf tied to the end.

"When I wave the scarf downward," he explained to the five girls who had lined up, "you start."

The skaters got set, waited breathlessly for a moment, then when the scarf swept downward, they were off! Their skates flashed in the sunlight as they raced toward the finish line some distance down the lake.

After the first few minutes it became apparent that the race was between Nellie Parks and Nan Bobbsey. When they were only a few yards from the boy who held another scarf to indicate the end of the race, they were almost even.

Then something happened. From the corner of her eye Nan saw Nellie slow down, then stop. Nan flashed across the finish line, the winner!

But as nearby skaters cheered, Nan turned back toward her friend. "What was the matter, Nellie?" she asked. "Why did you stop?"

"My lace broke," Nellie replied ruefully. "My foot was wobbling, and I couldn't go on!"

"The race wasn't fair then," Nan observed. "Let's do it again."

Although Nellie protested that she had been beaten fairly, Nan insisted that they race again. So once more they sped over the course. This time, too, the race was close, but Nan finished about a foot ahead of Nellie.

The other children gathered around and congratulated the skaters, then wandered off to watch other contests. Nan and Bert sat down on a heavy log near shore to rest awhile.

"It's going to be crowded driving to Snow Lodge," Nan said presently.

"Sure is," agreed Bert. "Eight of us. Sam and Dinah won't be along because they're going to visit some relatives over the holidays. But with all the luggage, Freddie's fire engine, Christmas presents, and Snap—"

"Don't forget Snoop," said Nan, and then remembered that Snoop was going to be left at the lumberyard with the foreman there. Mrs. Bobbsey had been afraid the cat might run off and get lost in the woods.

Bert was quiet for a moment, then suddenly he snapped his fingers. "Nan, I've got it! Why don't you and I and Harry and Dorothy sail our iceboat up to Snow Lodge? We can go all the way along Lake Metoka!"

Bert, with Charlie Mason's help, had recently built a very speedy iceboat, with a tall sail, they called the *Icebird,* out of material from Mr. Bobbsey's lumberyard. The two older twins had frequently enjoyed short excursions in the craft, but the journey to Snow Lodge at the far end of the lake would be the longest they had attempted.

"Oh, Bert!" Nan exclaimed. "That's a wonderful idea! I'm sure we could manage it. Let's ask Mother and Dad as soon as we see them."

At four-thirty the twins left the pond and headed for the railroad station. Mrs. Bobbsey was there with the car and they hopped in beside her. While the three waited for the train, Bert asked his mother about the trip in the *Icebird*.

She did not reply at once, then asked, "You feel sure you could manage such a long trip?"

"Oh, yes, Mother," Bert said quickly. "Harry's strong, and Nan and Dorothy are swell sailors."

"And you're pretty neat on ice," Nan put in, giggling.

Mrs. Bobbsey smiled. "We'll ask your father. I think it's all right, but on this you'll have to get his approval."

The twins hugged their pretty mother, then Nan said, "Here comes the train!"

She and Bert climbed out of the car and hurried through the station to the front platform. The train thundered in and stopped.

"I see her!" Nan cried, catching a glimpse of Dorothy Minturn standing at the door of a coach. She ran forward and waited at the steps for her cousin to come down.

The twelve-year-old, dark-haired girl was smiling broadly. "Hi, kids!" she called out. She gave Nan a kiss and Bert a vigorous handshake that twisted him in a half-circle. "How are you, old-timer? Say, isn't this simply super duper? You must tell me everything about Snow Lodge. And say, is Harry here?"

"He's coming, and, Dorothy, we might go up in the iceboat," Bert said.

"Terrific!" Dorothy replied.

The three children hurried to the station wagon. As Bert put Dorothy's bulging suitcase in, the visitor hugged her Aunt Mary. "You're wonderful to include me in the trip," she said. "Mother and Dad sent their love and some Christmas presents. They're in my bag." Dorothy giggled. "I mean the presents are. That's why it's so fat."

Mrs. Bobbsey laughed. "It's good to have you with us," she said. "Played any more tricks lately?" Dorothy Minturn was known for her joking.

"N-no," Dorothy replied. "But someone played an awfully mean one on me."

"How come?" Bert queried.

Dorothy made a face. "I was in a horse show. A horrid boy switched the numbers on my horse and another. It was announced that the blue ribbon would go to number five. That was my number and was I excited! But when I went up to get the ribbon, the mix-up was found out. Then I was burned up!"

"How awful!" cried Nan.

"Did you get anything?" Bert asked.

"Yes. Second place."

"And the mean boy? How about him?"

"He didn't win anything, and he was disqualified from riding in the rest of the show," Dorothy answered.

"Served him right," said Bert.

Soon after the group had arrived home, Mr. Bobbsey came in with Harry Bobbsey, whom he had met at the corner. There was a warm welcome for the tall farm boy who, winter and summer, had a deep tan and red cheeks.

"It's sure good to see you," said Bert. "I need another boy to protect me from all these girls!"

As the other laughed, Freddie piped up, "I'm here."

"Sure you are," Bert said, "and not afraid of anything."

"Of course not."

"Dad," said Bert, "how about letting Harry and Dorothy and Nan and me sail up to Snow Lodge in the *Icebird* tomorrow? Then you won't be so crowded in the station wagon."

Mr. Bobbsey was thoughtful a few moments, then asked, "Have you mentioned it to Mother?" He smiled. "We like to do our worrying together, you know. Personally, I think you can manage the trip."

"Oh, Mother has already said okay if it's all right with you," Bert answered quickly. "Thanks, Dad."

"I want to be part of the crew!" Freddie put in excitedly.

"And I'll be dee-lighted to go," Flossie added. The little girl jumped up and down and clapped her hands. "Oh, please. It would be fun!"

Mrs. Bobbsey put her arms around the younger twins. "I'm sorry, children," she said, "but I'm afraid that's not wise. The iceboat can be tricky to handle, and I don't think you've had enough experience.

"Besides," she added with a twinkle in her eyes, "who'll help Dad and me with Snap and the luggage if you're on the *Icebird*?"

"And there really isn't room," Nan added.

The young twins thought about this for a minute and then reluctantly agreed that they would save their rides in the *Icebird* until later.

"But I wouldn't be afraid," Freddie declared, "not even if—not even if a bear came out of the woods after us!"

The others laughed, then the older twins and their cousins went upstairs with the luggage.

Soon Dinah sounded the gong announcing that supper was ready. The family assembled and Mr. Bobbsey said grace. Then the chatter began. All during the meal the proposed trip was discussed. The cousins were told about the breakdown of the furnace.

"It's only working feebly," said Mrs. Bobbsey. "I'll be glad to live again in a warm house."

Finally, as everyone finished eating, she pushed back her chair and stood up. "We may as well go into the living room," she said. "Freddie and Bert, how about building a fire? It's pretty chilly."

Harry helped, and soon they had a cheery fire going. The family gathered around it, and began to check over what food, clothing, and sports equipment was already packed for their holiday.

"It sounds like enough," Mr. Bobbsey said, smiling. "The poor station wagon will be groaning."

Freddie laughed but said, "We might get snowed in. Let's take plenty to eat!"

Nan smiled. "If that happened we might not be able to return to school in time."

The small boy's eyes danced mischievously. "That's all right with me!" he exclaimed, and everyone grinned.

Bert jingled some change in his pants pocket and said, "Wouldn't it be swell if we could find Mr. Carford's missing money?"

Nodding eagerly, Nan said, "Think how happy he would be! Then he and his nephew could be friends again and return to live in Snow Lodge."

Quickly she told Dorothy and Harry about the trouble between Mr. Carford and his nephew.

Flossie took a deep breath and said, "But let's not find the money right away—'cause if we do

we might have to move out so Mr. Carford and
his nephew could move back into the lodge—
and I want to have some fun there for a while!"
she ended breathlessly.

Mr. Bobbsey threw back his head and
laughed. Finally he managed to say, "Honey, if
the police couldn't find the money—not even a
clue to it—you don't have to worry about *when*
you'll find it. The question is *if!*"

Flossie smiled sheepishly and agreed. Then
she got up from her pillow on the floor by the
fireplace. "I'm going upstairs. I must see if my
dolly's snow clothes are ready for her vacation,"
she announced importantly.

Freddie, too, wandered off to the room he
shared with Bert. A minute later the others heard
him give a wild cry. He came pounding down the
stairs and raced into the living room, wild-eyed.

"It's in my room! A-a great big bear. He
growled at me, and his eyes—they're—they're
real big and shiny!"

CHAPTER IX

THE MYSTERIOUS NOTE

"A BEAR!" Harry cried out. "How did he get in the house?"

"I—I don't know," Freddie answered.

By this time Mr. Bobbsey and Bert were dashing up the stairs two steps at a time, with Nan at their heels. Reaching the boys' room they could indeed see two bright-glaring eyes in a corner of the room. A moment later there came a low growl.

"Oh!" the three exclaimed.

Mr. Bobbsey switched on the light. Everyone stared in blank amazement, then burst into laughter. There was a bear in the room all right —but a toy bear with electrically lighted eyes. In a chair sat Dorothy Minturn, growling merrily.

By this time Freddie had arrived and was peering into the room between his father's legs. "You meanie!" he exclaimed, but laughed as he walked in.

"Why, Freddie," said Dorothy, pretending to be hurt, "how can you say such a thing? Here I lugged this nice bear all the way from home to give you for Christmas, and now I guess you don't want it."

Freddie managed a crestfallen grin. "I won't say again I'm not afraid of anything. It was pretty silly being afraid of a toy bear. Thanks a lot, Dorothy. I like him."

As Freddie went over to try turning the electric eyes on and off, the others went downstairs and continued their discussion about the holiday trip.

"We'll cut our own Christmas tree in the woods," Mr. Bobbsey said. "And trim it with things you can make yourselves."

"How about strings of popcorn?" Nan suggested.

"Mm, popcorn," said Harry. "Some would taste good right now."

"We'll make some," Nan suggested. "Come on." She led the way into the kitchen, where Dinah was bustling about. "May we roast some popcorn?" she asked the cook.

"Why, sure you can, honey child!" Dinah answered. "Matter of fact I was just thinkin' the same thing myself."

At this moment Sam Johnson came in from outside. He greeted the visiting cousins, who, like the twins, adored Dinah's tall, easygoing husband. "I'll get the popper," he offered. "It's down in the basement."

Presently Dinah and Sam went upstairs to their room. The twins found boxes of corn, and soon the merry *pop pop* of the grains could be heard. Nan melted some butter and was just about to take it from the stove when the children were alarmed by the sound of several bumps, then a crash on the stairway in the hall.

"Susie!" they heard Flossie scream.

A second later a louder *bumpety, bump, bump, crash!* rang through the house, followed by a moan.

"Flossie!" Mrs. Bobbsey cried, darting into the hall with the rest of the family following.

In a crumpled heap on the hall rug lay the little girl. Her doll was in a grotesque position on the bottom step. Alarmed, Mrs. Bobbsey bent over Flossie and quickly, but gently, examined her carefully.

"Darling, are you hurt?" she asked, as her young daughter's eyes fluttered open.

Flossie tried to sit upright. "I—I don't know yet," she gasped. Then, getting to her feet, she said:

"My dolly—she fell and I tried to reach her and—" Flossie caught sight of the doll. "Oh, Susie, are you all right?"

She picked up the toy and cuddled it close, as Mr. Bobbsey caught up both of them.

"Hey, little fat fairy," he said, smiling to hide his worry. "Are you sure nothing is wrong?"

"Honest, Daddy, I'm okay 'cept I bumped my knee and right elbow. But I'm afraid Susie's hurt bad."

"Let's see if Susie can still walk," suggested Nan. Taking the doll from Flossie, Nan walked a few paces with the doll's feet touching the floor.

As Dinah and Sam hurried down the stairs to see what had caused the noise, Flossie heaved a sigh of relief and, taking the doll back, began to talk to Susie.

Suddenly she turned to her mother with tears in her eyes. "Susie's lost her voice!" she cried in despair. "She can't say a word—not even 'Mama'!"

Sobbing, Flossie crouched on the bottom step and rocked the doll back and forth in her arms.

Sam sat down beside Flossie. "Here now," he said kindly, "let me see Susie. Maybe I can fix her for you."

"Oh, could you, Sam?" said Flossie, her eyes shining hopefully through her tears. Tenderly she laid the doll in the man's outstretched hands.

Sam placed the doll face down on his lap, then rummaged about in his pockets until he produced a tiny screwdriver. Next he removed a small plate on the doll's back, made some adjustments inside, and replaced the plate.

With a wink at Flossie, Sam turned Susie right side up again. "Good morning, Mama!" Susie said in a high-pitched voice.

"Oh, Sam, you cured her!" Flossie squealed, smiling at him as she hugged the doll tight. "Thank you, and Susie does, too. You're a real doll-doctor!"

"Hey!" Bert interrupted, sniffing the air. "What's burning?"

"Oh, good night!" Nan cried, racing toward the kitchen. "It's the butter I was melting for the popcorn!"

The saucepan was black and the butter had disappeared completely. Smoke hung in the air. Bert turned on the ventilating fan, while Nan found another pan and put in a new chunk of butter.

"It's a good thing your popper is automatic or the corn would have burned, too," Dorothy remarked, as she picked up the burned saucepan to scour it.

Harry chuckled. "Never a dull moment!"

Half an hour later as the whole family was enjoying a fresh batch of buttered popcorn, the telephone rang.

Bert hurried to answer it, and they could hear him say, "Yes, we're leaving tomorrow morning. We'll be there a week. Oh, that's all right. Good-by."

When Bert returned to the fireplace his mother asked who had called.

"A man from the newspaper. He said the *Lakeport Times* wanted to put a line in the social column about our trip."

Mrs. Bobbsey frowned. "A man?" she said. "Why, the social page is run by Clara Estes. I know her well. No man has anything to do with the social news."

"I'm sorry, Mother," said Bert. "I didn't know—"

"Of course you didn't," Mrs. Bobbsey broke in. "But recently burglars have been using the telephone method to learn when people will be away."

Bert was greatly worried. "I'll never do such a thing again. Maybe we should notify the police."

"I think we should," Mr. Bobbsey agreed. "I'll ask them to keep an eye on the house until we get back."

He went to the phone at once and put in the call. The police captain promised that patrol cars and a special detective would be on hand to protect the property and also to nab any burglar who might come there.

"I feel better now," said Bert, heaving a sigh of relief. "I sure muffed that one."

Mrs. Bobbsey smiled. "I feel better about it, too. And now, how about bed for you children? The earlier you wake up, the earlier we can get started for Snow Lodge."

"I s'pose so," said Flossie, "but I hate to leave this nice fire. I just know my bed's going to be freezing cold."

"Mine, too," Freddie added. "Please, Mommy, may we have our bedtime story down here?"

"All right," Mrs. Bobbsey agreed, "and everyone can take part in the telling. I'll start and we'll go around the circle, with each one continuing where the other leaves off."

"Dorothy, don't you play any more tricks," Freddie pleaded.

His cousin grinned. "Not a real one, anyway," she promised.

Mrs. Bobbsey began. "Once upon a time there was a large family who lived in a lovely house in the woods."

"That's us—starting tomorrow," Flossie interrupted.

"Soon it began to snow," her mother went on, "and by the next morning the snow was so deep that— Harry, go on with the story."

"So deep that the only way the people could get out was from the second-floor windows," said Harry. "One boy named Bert tried it and went right down in the fluffy stuff all the way to the ground."

"Oh!" cried Flossie. "Did somebody rescue him?"

Harry grinned. "Bert crawled under the snow toward a cellar window that he knew was open, and—" The storyteller turned to Nan. "Your turn."

"Just as Bert felt as if he couldn't hold his breath another second, he climbed in and was safe."

"I'm so glad," Flossie murmured.

At that moment the front door chimes sounded. "I'll go," Bert offered, and went into the hall.

After he opened the door, there was silence. A moment later the family heard Bert gasp. Then he closed the door quickly and returned to the living room. He was holding an envelope and a sheet of paper from which he was reading with a puzzled frown.

"What does it say?" his father asked.

"I found this under the door. But there wasn't anybody on the porch or anywhere in sight."

"What does it say?" Mr. Bobbsey repeated.

Bert wore a frightened, puzzled expression on his face. Then, as all eyes were on him, he said, "It—it's addressed to the Bobbsey twins. It says:

'Stay away from Snow Lodge! If you don't, you'll be sorry. The Black Monster will get you all!' "

CHAPTER X

TRICKS

"B-BLACK Monster!" Freddie whispered as Bert gave his father the note to read. The little boy's whole body was tense with fright.

Flossie gasped and grabbed her mother, who was seated next to her on the sofa.

Mr. Bobbsey examined the coarse white paper. Then suddenly he chuckled. "Don't be frightened, children," he said. "There's no such thing as a 'Black Monster.' One of your friends is playing a joke on you. I think a child wrote this note."

Instantly all eyes turned on Dorothy. But the girl who loved to play jokes declared she had had nothing to do with this one. "You know I wasn't out of this room, so how could I have sounded the chimes?"

"You didn't get someone to do it for you?" Harry put in.

"No, and why should I?" Dorothy was becoming a little indignant. "I want to go to Snow Lodge as much as anybody."

"Sorry," said Harry. "Uncle Dick, do you think it could have anything to do with the phone call from that man who wanted to know when we were leaving?"

If Mr. Bobbsey thought so, he did not admit it. Instead, looking at Freddie and Flossie, he said, "Now which one of your playmates might play such a trick?"

"I know just which one—Danny Rugg!" Bert exclaimed. "Don't you see," he said to Flossie and Freddie, "this practically has Danny's name written all over it."

"The note does sound like the type of prank Danny plays," admitted Mrs. Bobbsey, stroking Flossie's hand.

"I agree," said Nan. "Remember his threat to 'fix the Bobbseys'? Well, the note is probably Danny's idea of how to do it. Let's spoil his plan by not letting on we care one bit."

Suddenly Bert snapped his fingers. "In fact, I'll bet I can prove that Danny wrote this silly thing. One of the fellows in our class passed around a sheet of paper the other day, and everybody wrote a little poem on it—a sort of Christmas greeting to our teachers. Remember, Nan?"

"Yes, and I brought the poems home and copied them in green ink on a piece of red Christmas paper," his twin added. "The original sheet is still on the desk in my bedroom. Wait a second. I'll get it."

In a few minutes Nan was back, holding the sheet of notebook paper on which there were a number of handwritten verses. The older twins rapidly scanned the paper until they came to the one signed by Danny Rugg.

"Here it is," Bert said. A queer look came over his face, then he chuckled. "Danny's not much of a poet. He wrote, 'Christmas comes but once a year and are we glad when it gets here.' "

Nan laughed and added, "Well, I guess we'd all better get to bed."

Instantly Mrs. Bobbsey, knowing something was wrong, literally scooped up Freddie and Flossie and whisked them upstairs.

After they were safely out of earshot, Bert said, "Dad, this note wasn't written by Danny. And it looks like a man's handwriting, anyway."

Mr. Bobbsey looked at Nan and Bert proudly. "You two played your parts well in front of Freddie and Flossie. I'm afraid some man did write this note. But who and why?"

"Do you think," Nan asked, "that it could be Dave Burdock, Mr. Carford's nephew?"

"Not a chance. He's too fine a man," Mr. Bobbsey replied.

"This is more of a mystery than I expected," said Harry. He stood up, crouched over, and doubled up his fists. "Okay, Black Monster, do your stuff, and see how long you last!"

The others laughed and soon the four children said good night and went upstairs. Harry was bunking in with the boys on an extra cot, while Dorothy had the guest room. As Mrs. Bobbsey came to see that all of them were comfortable, she whispered to each one:

"No matter who wrote that note, I don't want any of you children to pay any more attention to it or worry. Obviously it's someone's idea of a joke, whether he's a boy or a man."

The next morning everyone was up early and busy scurrying around before breakfast. While Nan helped her mother pack last-minute articles in suitcases, Dorothy assisted Flossie in wrapping Christmas packages. There were many secret conferences and much giggling and rustling of gift paper.

Mr. Bobbsey and Harry packed the station wagon. Meanwhile, Bert and Freddie took Snoop to the lumberyard foreman.

"This is our Black Monster," said Freddie with a chuckle, then quickly leaned over and gave Snoop a big hug in case his feelings were hurt.

After listening to Freddie describe the exact temperature of the milk and just what each meal should consist of, the foreman threw up his hands and cried:

"Whoa there, son! On that diet, your cat will be so fat when you folks get back he won't be able to squeeze through your front door!"

Freddie grinned good-naturedly and gave Snoop a parting pat. The boys hurried home and all the family sat down to a sumptuous breakfast.

"I just thought you sailors ought to feed up strong," Dinah said with a grin. "You got a long journey in that iceboat. And I fixed you a little snack in case the wind dies down and you find you're stuck for a while."

"Oh, that's sweet of you," said Nan with a big smile.

The other "sailors" nodded. "Nifty." "Super." "Swell," they said.

Breakfast started with orange juice and stewed prunes. Then came oatmeal, and finally sausage and griddle cakes with syrup, and milk.

During a pause in the conversation, a squeaky voice suddenly said from a corner of the dining room, "Aren't you going to take me?"

Everyone looked up, startled. In the corner, seated on a child's chair, was one of Flossie's dolls, but no human being.

"Please take me along," the doll seemed to say.

Flossie's eyes opened wide. "But Janie's not a talking doll," she said, puzzled. "How could she—"

Suddenly all eyes turned on Dorothy. "Did you say that? Are you playing another trick?" Flossie demanded.

Dorothy laughed. "Not guilty. Honest."

"Then who—" Nan asked, looking from one to another at the table.

Nobody answered her, but Harry said, "How about Dinah?"

At this instant the jolly cook came into the room with another plate stacked high with griddle cakes. She was smiling.

"Dinah, did you make my dolly talk?" Flossie asked her.

Dinah's smile changed to a puzzled frown. "Did I what? Of course not, honey child."

At this very instant the doll said, "I'll freeze here with no heat."

"Of course you will," said Flossie. "I'll take you along and Diane and Jill and—"

Just then Bert burst out laughing. He pushed back his chair, stood up, and holding out his hand toward Harry, said:

"Ladies and gentlemen, you have just been listening to the voice of one of the country's youngest and most talented ventriloquists—Harry Bobbsey of Meadowbrook!"

"You!" Nan exclaimed. "Why, Harry, you're really good. How'd you learn to throw your voice and fool us like that?"

Harry grinned. "I sent for a book, and I've

been practicing. So I'm good, eh? You're my first audience."

"I'll say you're good," Dorothy praised him. "The rest of us had better watch our step at Snow Lodge."

Mr. Bobbsey chuckled. "With Dorothy's tricks and Harry's ventriloquism, I'm not sure how we Lakeport Bobbseys will come out on this vacation."

Mrs. Bobbsey thought they should start, so coats, caps, mittens, and boots were put on. Mr. Bobbsey said he would drive the four older children to the lake, then return for the others.

As they neared the *Icebird's* dock Bert noticed a figure climb off the boat and walk rapidly away. He wondered who it was, and decided it was just someone interested in iceboats.

"Say, this is a honey!" Harry exclaimed as the children piled out of the station wagon. Each carried his skates, so in case of an accident to the *Icebird* they could skate to Snow Lodge.

Dorothy agreed enthusiastically about the boat. Nan explained that she and Bert called the craft *Icebird* because it almost seemed to fly over the ice.

When Bert, Nan, and their cousins were aboard, Mr. Bobbsey shoved them off. The sail was unfurled and a sharp breeze caught it. Soon the little craft was skimming smoothly over the ice in the direction of Snow Lodge.

On shore Mr. Bobbsey waved and called, "Good luck!" until the *Icebird* rounded a bend in the shoreline and disappeared.

Then he drove back to the Bobbsey home where Mrs. Bobbsey and the small twins were

waiting. Freddie hopped into the front seat with his father while Mrs. Bobbsey, Flossie, and Snap got in back.

"Now do we have everything?" Mr. Bobbsey asked, wanting to be sure nothing had been forgotten.

Mrs. Bobbsey nodded reassuringly, but Freddie asked, "How about my fire engine? Is it in here, Daddy?" His father assured him it was.

"And Susie!" Flossie cried. "Where's my dolly?"

"Snap is sitting on her," Mrs. Bobbsey said with a chuckle. Flossie retrieved the doll at once and straightened her clothes.

"We're off!" Freddie exclaimed. Snap barked in excitement, and Sam and Dinah waved good-by from the front porch.

Meanwhile, the older children were enjoying their brisk pace on the ice. The wind held steady, filling the sail, but keeping the iceboat's speed under control. At first Bert and Harry took turns at the rudder, but when the girls wanted to, Bert let each of them steer for a while.

"Oh, this is fun!" Nan exclaimed, her cheeks pink from the wind and her brown hair blowing softly. "I'm so thrilled you two could come with us," she said, smiling at Dorothy and Harry. "It's just making a perfect Christmas week."

"Maybe you think I'm not glad!" Harry cried, and Dorothy agreed enthusiastically.

Soon the conversation turned to the Black Monster and the mystery of Snow Lodge.

"What do you figure it means?" Nan asked.

Harry was inclined to think the two were not connected. Dorothy felt sure the Black Monster business was a gag and they would hear no more about it.

"Danny Rugg could have had somebody else write the note," she said.

"That's true," Nan agreed.

"Just the same," Bert said, "I have a hunch there *is* a connection between the Black Monster warning and the strange story about Snow Lodge. I just can't wait to get there to find out."

All the children were eager to arrive at the locked-up house in the woods. "We're making good time," Harry remarked.

Nan, who was at the tiller, looked a little worried. "A little too fast," she said. "The wind's getting strong and sort of tricky. Maybe you'd better do the steering for a while, Bert."

She turned the rudder over to her twin and looked anxiously at the sky. The wind was freshening fast. Then it began to come in sudden gusts, shrieking in the bellying sail. Harry joined Bert at the rudder. The girls clung to the mast as the *Icebird* veered crazily from side to side.

"Hold on tight, everybody!" Bert shouted over the roar of the gale. "We'll try to ride it out!"

At that moment there was a sharp crack! The mainsheet snapped. The sail whipped wildly for a moment, then swung about.

Completely out of control, the iceboat tipped over, scattering the four youngsters in every direction over the windswept ice of Lake Metoka!

CHAPTER XI

THE "ICEBIRD" IN TROUBLE

THE cries of the children, as they slid over the ice, were lost in the howling wind.

Suddenly Nan felt a thud through her whole body and found she had been slammed against a dock. She got up cautiously, still clinging to one of the pilings, and was glad to find she had not been injured.

"Bert! Harry! Dorothy!" she called. There was no answer. Nan's heart sank.

As she looked around fearfully, Nan noticed that the gale had died as suddenly as it had come up. The slate-gray clouds had passed over and a feeble ray of sunlight shone on the ice.

"Nan! Nan!" Bert called as he struggled toward the overturned iceboat. Where are you?"

"Over here," his twin answered and waved from the dock.

Turning around, she was surprised to see Dorothy clinging to another piling at the far end. "Are you all right?" she called to her cousin.

"Just a little battered," the girl answered cheerfully. "How are the others?"

In reply Nan pointed toward the *Icebird*. Harry and Bert were struggling to right it. The two girls made their way over to the boat, and in a few minutes the four children had pulled it to the dock.

"Whew!" Bert gasped. "That was some experience. It's a lucky thing none of us was hurt!"

"What happened?" Harry asked.

"I don't know," Bert admitted. "Let's see if we can find out."

Carefully the two boys examined the mainsheet which had snapped in the gale, causing the craft to tip over.

Suddenly Bert exclaimed, "This line was cut! Sliced almost halfway through! See?" He held up both ends of the rope, pointing out that only half the strands had frayed apart. The others had obviously been cut. "I can't understand why I didn't notice it before we started!"

"Somebody did this deliberately," Harry said grimly. "But who?"

Bert dropped the rope and looked up. "Good night!" he exclaimed. "It must have been the guy I saw getting off the boat!"

"What do you mean, Bert?" Nan asked. "When did you see anybody?"

Her brother told them about the figure he had seen running from the iceboat as they drove up.

"What did he look like?" Dorothy asked.

"We were too far away for me to see that," Bert explained. "He was medium height and had on a black coat and cap."

"Perhaps it was the Black Monster!" Nan exclaimed.

"Well, he really *is* a monster to cut that rope on the *Icebird*," Dorothy remarked indignantly.

"Of course having the line break wouldn't have been too dangerous if it hadn't been for that heavy wind," Bert countered. "Why do you suppose he did it?"

"To keep us from going to Snow Lodge!" Dorothy exclaimed.

"He can't do that," Bert replied determinedly. "Come on, Harry, let's splice the mainsheet right now. The *Icebird* seems perfectly all right otherwise."

With fingers stiff from the cold, the boys took more than fifteen minutes to repair the line. Nan and Dorothy chased one another around the dock to keep warm.

When the splicing job was finally completed, Nan made a suggestion. "Why don't we see if we can make a fire, then have the sandwiches and doughnuts and hot chocolate that Dinah gave us?"

"Great," Harry agreed. "I'm about frozen!"

The children scurried about accumulating stray sticks of dry wood and in a short while had a small fire going. "Boy! This feels good," Bert commented as he stretched his cold hands toward the blaze.

Nan opened the box of sandwiches and passed it around while Dorothy poured the steaming cocoa into paper cups.

"Mm yum," Harry remarked as he bit into a cheese sandwich. "Now I'll be able to make it to Snow Lodge!"

When they had finished the doughnuts and the last drop of cocoa, Nan stood up. "How about skating, Dorothy?" she suggested. "We ought to be able to keep up with the boat for a while. We can climb aboard again when we get tired."

Dorothy nodded enthusiastically, and the girls laced on their skates. Bert and Harry shoved the boat off and hopped aboard.

"Let's see if we can make the *Icebird* outrun them," Bert whispered to Harry.

Grinning, Harry nodded and took over the tiller. Soon the little craft began to pick up speed. Nan and Dorothy skated faster and faster trying to keep up. But little by little they fell behind.

Finally Nan called. "You win! Slow down so we can come aboard!"

The boys hove to, and the girls climbed onto the deck. "Wow!" Dorothy cried. "I think I'd just as soon ride the rest of the way!"

A short while later Bert glanced uneasily at the western horizon where dark, menacing clouds were gathering rapidly. "Looks like another storm," he remarked. "I hope we can make Snow Lodge before it breaks. The house can't be too far from here."

For a few minutes it looked as if they might be able to reach the lodge ahead of the storm. The rising wind bellied the *Icebird's* sail and sent the craft whizzing over the ice much faster than before. But the skies continued to darken, and soon Nan felt a snowflake on her cheek.

With astonishing speed, the snowfall thickened until the shoreline was only a hazy line seen through the wind-driven flakes. Desperately Bert and Harry peered ahead, straining their eyes to keep the shore in view so the craft could hold on course.

Huddled together with their backs to the wind, Nan and Dorothy were too cold and worried to say a word. Soon the snow was like a thick cotton veil, covering the boat and shutting out all sound. Gradually the wind slackened and the *Icebird* slowed to a turtle's pace.

"I can't see the shore!" Bert shouted. "But I guess it doesn't matter. The snow's so thick on the ice that the runners are beginning to get bogged down."

"And now the wind's almost gone," Harry added. "Looks as if we're marooned, kids."

Nan tried to remain calm. "Can't we go the rest of the way to Snow Lodge on foot, Bert?" she asked. "We must be almost there."

"We'll have to try," Bert agreed in a grim voice. "Everybody over the side. We'll haul the *Icebird* to shore and tie her up."

The children pulled on the boat's mooring line steadily, knowing the shore could not be far away. Soon they spotted a stump and lashed the craft fast, then furled the sail.

"Now," Bert said encouragingly, stamping his cold feet, "if we hug the shoreline and just keep going, we're bound to find Snow Lodge."

Nan and Dorothy nodded gamely, suppressing shivers. The air had grown bitter during the past half-hour and seemed chillier with every passing moment.

"Bert, you lead the way, then Nan and Dorothy follow," Harry directed. "I'll bring up the rear. Let's go—one, two, three, march!" he shouted cheerfully, trying to sound like an army sergeant.

A few minutes later the wind picked up again, hurling its cargo of snow at the struggling children. They had to bend almost double to keep their balance, and progress seemed impossible at times.

"Any sign of the lodge, Bert?" Harry shouted. But the howling wind swept away his words, and they all plodded along silently.

Finally, blinded by the stinging flakes and half frozen, the children huddled together behind a fallen tree trunk away from the wind. "We'll rest here a minute, then go on," Bert gasped.

Nan's fingers and feet were numb, and she knew the others were equally miserable. The snow was like a heavy white blanket which seemed to smother them.

"Will we ever find Snow Lodge in this storm?" Dorothy murmured.

"We'll freeze if we stay here," Harry said after a few minutes. "We'll have to start on if we're ever going to find Snow Lodge."

"Yes, we must hurry," Nan agreed. "And I'll bet Mother and Dad will be terribly worried about us in this storm."

The four scrambled to their feet and resumed plodding single file through the blinding snowstorm. Trying to follow the shoreline, they were forced to scramble over rocks and detour around fallen trees.

A little later Dorothy broke the silence to exclaim, "I think the snow's letting up a little. I can make out things ahead more easily."

Raising their heads, the others saw that Dorothy was right. Wearily they stumbled on, but now with a tiny spark of hope to warm them.

Fifteen minutes passed. Then Nan gave a sharp cry and sat down in the snow with such suddenness that Harry, walking behind her, nearly fell over her. Bert and Dorothy turned back.

"What's the matter, sis?" Bert asked anxiously.

"I—I've got a Charlie horse in my leg," Nan said with a wince. "What a time to have this happen!"

"Try to stand up," Dorothy suggested. "Maybe it will work out."

Nan struggled to her feet, grimacing with pain. She stamped on her foot to get rid of the cramp in her leg. But it did no good. Finally

Bert and Harry, although their hands were numb with cold, massaged her leg enough to relieve the muscle tension and to stir up the circulation.

"It's better now," Nan said in relief. "I think I can go on all right."

With Bert in the lead again they struggled on, each one concentrating only on putting one foot ahead of the other.

Suddenly Dorothy gave a happy cry. "A light! I see one through the trees!"

CHAPTER XII

THE TREE'S BIRTHDAY CANDLES

AT DOROTHY'S cry the others stopped and peered ahead. There *was* a light, dimmed considerably by the falling snow, but still easily seen. It was about twenty yards ahead and perhaps thirty to their left, back among the trees.

"That must be it!" Bert cried. "Snow Lodge!"

The children floundered through the snow toward the light. The distance seemed so great! They felt as if they had traveled miles before seeing the dim outline of a large house.

As the children reached the front door, Bert pounded on it, calling, "Mother! Dad!"

The door opened, and a broad beam of warm yellow light shone across the snow. The next moment Nan gave a sob of relief—Mr. and Mrs. Bobbsey were silhouetted in the doorway! She ran forward. But then, more tired than she realized, she slipped on an icy patch and crumpled in the snow.

Instantly Mr. Bobbsey rushed out and caught Nan up in his arms and hurried inside. Mrs. Bobbsey, with a fervent "Thank goodness, you are here at last!" urged the other three children to hasten indoors.

Fifteen minutes later the children, in dry clothes, were seated in front of a roaring fire in

the living room, drinking hot lemonade which Mrs. Bobbsey had hurriedly prepared for them.

"Don't try to tell us what happened," Mrs. Bobbsey cautioned. "Just rest until I have supper ready. Then we can all hear your story together."

"Isn't this a lovely place!" Nan exclaimed, gazing around at the enormous living room.

A wall of fieldstone formed one long side and contained the five-foot-square fireplace opening. Above it stretched a wide walnut mantel. French doors opened onto a terrace at the far end. The high ceiling was supported by large, hand-hewn walnut beams.

"I'd love to live here," Dorothy remarked, admiring the hand-hooked rugs, the paneled walls, and the comfortable, dark red leather furniture.

"Let's start our search for the missing money right after supper," Bert suggested with an eager look.

By the time Mrs. Bobbsey brought in a steaming hot supper which she set on a table in one corner of the room, the four children were feeling rested. They ate hungrily and eagerly told of their adventure in the storm.

Freddie and Flossie listened wide-eyed, and Freddie sighed as he said, "I wish I'd been there!"

"I don't!" Flossie said energetically. "It makes me cold just to listen!"

Mr. Bobbsey said he had been getting ready to organize a search party for the missing children when he heard Bert pounding on the door.

"The rest of us arrived here in good time," Mr. Bobbsey explained, "and were busy unpacking and looking around the lodge. We didn't realize it was snowing so hard."

Supper finished, the children helped Mrs. Bobbsey with the dishes. Then Bert again suggested a tour of the house and a search for the missing money.

Mr. and Mrs. Bobbsey looked at each other and grinned. "You children certainly have boundless energy. Go ahead," Mrs. Bobbsey said. "But we'll set a time limit so you can get a good night's sleep. You may search for one hour."

"Come on, kids, let's get started," Bert urged. He took a flashlight from the mantel.

The four children, followed by Flossie and Freddie, walked slowly around the spacious living room. They examined the floors for trap doors and knocked on the paneled walls for signs of secret passageways or hollow spots.

Coming to a door at the end of the fireplace wall, Dorothy asked, "Where does this lead?"

"To the den. That part of the house is only one story high," Freddie explained, proud of his knowledge. "Go on in."

What a fascinating room it was! Deerskins,

old rifles, powder horns, mounted fish, and a huge moosehead decorated the walls. Before a hearth lay as large a bear rug as any the children had ever seen. They made a careful search of the room but found no signs of any hiding place which might contain the lost money.

"Our time is almost up," Nan observed. "Let's take a quick look at the kitchen."

Almost one entire side of this room was taken up by a huge, walk-in fireplace of stone. Old iron pots hung from cranes, the same as had been used in olden days.

"Isn't this exciting?" Nan said enthusiastically as she stepped into the fireplace and peered up the old chimney. As she turned to come back into the room an iron ring in the wall caught her eye. "I wonder—" she mused. She took hold of the rusty ring and pulled.

Slowly a door opened!

"Bert! Dorothy! Harry!" she called. "I've found something!"

The others came running and crowded into the fireplace. Bert beamed his flashlight carefully into the space where the door had been. It showed a flight of steps leading downward.

At this moment Mrs. Bobbsey came into the kitchen to tell the children their hour for searching was up. "Okay, Mother," said Nan. "We've made a big discovery tonight and tomorrow we'll see where this tunnel leads!"

But when they gathered for breakfast the next morning, Mr. Bobbsey thought they had better change their plans.

"How about hiking back and getting the *Icebird* while the weather's good?" he proposed to the older children.

"Oh yes, we should, before somebody takes it," Bert agreed.

He and Nan, Dorothy, and Harry donned warm coats, boots, and mittens and climbed to the summit of a large, wooded hill not far from the lodge to see if they could spot the iceboat.

What a marvelous view stretched before them! Fields and deep forests and a few scattered houses met their gaze. The broad, flat expanse of white in the distance must surely be Lake Metoka.

"I think I see the *Icebird*!" Nan exclaimed. "Over there, about a mile from the lodge."

"A mile!" Dorothy groaned. "Last night it seemed more like a hundred miles!"

"It shouldn't be any trouble to get the boat and moor it nearer the house," Harry said. "Let's go!"

When they reached the abandoned craft a quick examination revealed that it had weathered the storm very well. With no wind to help them, it took the children a long time to drag the iceboat across the snow-covered lake to the dock at the lodge. But at last they had it tied fast.

"That's a good job done," Bert said with satisfaction, rubbing his hands together to warm them. "What do you suppose that little building is over there?" He pointed to a small stone house about a hundred yards from the lodge.

"Let's go and see," Nan proposed.

As they made their way over to the dilapidated-looking structure, they speculated as to its use. Pushing open the sagging door, they saw a dirt-covered floor. The ceiling was high, with long hooks hanging from the rafters.

"A smokehouse!" Harry cried. "We used to have one like this at Meadowbrook."

While the boys examined the hooks, Nan and Dorothy were scuffling around the floor. Suddenly Dorothy stumbled over something. It was another iron ring.

"Let's see if we can lift it," Nan suggested, leaning over and grasping the handle firmly. To her surprise it moved easily and a trap door raised up. A flight of steps ran down from it.

"These steps have been used recently!" Bert exclaimed. "I wonder if this connects with the tunnel starting from the lodge kitchen!"

Nan's brown eyes sparkled. "Dorothy and I will go back there and start through the tunnel. You and Harry go down these steps and we'll see if we meet!"

"Great! We'll give you five minutes' start!"

The two girls ran toward the lodge. When they explained their plan to Mrs. Bobbsey and the small twins, Freddie and Flossie insisted upon going into the tunnel with them.

"Be careful, children," Mrs. Bobbsey cautioned, as she handed Nan a large flashlight. "Call if you run into anything unusual. I'll stay right here in the kitchen."

"Yes, Mother," Nan agreed.

"Wow, it's dark!" Dorothy cried, peering over her cousin's shoulder, as Nan led the way down a narrow stairway, flashing the beam over walls and floor. After them came Freddie, then Flossie.

Stone walls, glistening with moisture, seemed to press in upon them. Cobwebs spread their silky touch over the children's faces, and a scurrying sound indicated that mice lived here.

"Ooh, it's spooky!" Flossie quavered.

Suddenly Nan stopped, turned off her flash, and held up a hand to warn the others. "I think I see a light beaming ahead," she whispered. "I— I hope it's Bert and Harry!"

Motionless and silent, the children watched a ray of light play on the walls, floor, and ceiling. Gradually it came nearer. Nan gasped as the beam flashed on her face.

"It's Nan!" she heard Harry cry triumphantly. Then he and Bert rushed up to join the others.

Nan laughed. "Even though I knew it must be you," she explained, "it was still scary!"

Excited over their discovery, the children went through the tunnel into the kitchen. All during lunch they discussed the secret tunnel. Why did it lead from the kitchen to the old smokehouse? And what had it been used for?

"We'll ask Mr. Carford the next time we see him," Nan said eagerly.

Bert spoke up. "Do you realize it's Christmas Eve? We have a lot to do this afternoon!"

Mr. Bobbsey agreed. "I think the first order of business for us men is to cut the Christmas tree!"

Bundling up well and carrying two axes from the tool house, Mr. Bobbsey, Bert, Freddie, and Harry set out.

As soon as they left, Nan and Dorothy began to pop corn to make strings of it to hang on the tree. Mrs. Bobbsey and Flossie assembled brightly colored cardboard and cans of water-color paint Flossie had found in a kitchen drawer.

For the next hour the little group busied themselves stringing the white corn puffs, painting walnut shells in gay colors, and cutting the cardboard into fantastic shapes. Soon they had a large pile of glittering tree ornaments.

"Oh, Flossie! Look at you!" her mother cried when they had finished. The little girl was liberally sprinkled with red and green dots which had splashed from her brush.

"I'm a Christmas tree ornament!" Flossie exclaimed, jumping up and running around the room waving her arms.

"That's right," Nan agreed teasingly. "We'll hang you on the top of the tree, and you can be the Christmas angel!"

"I'd rather be down with the rest of you," Flossie decided, "so I'll wash off the paint!"

The little girl scampered off. As she returned to the living room they heard pounding on the front door. When Nan opened it, the children beheld the largest spruce tree they had ever seen! It appeared to walk into the room by itself but behind it came Mr. Bobbsey and the boys, their faces glowing from the cold.

"That's bee-yoo-ti-ful, Daddy!" Flossie cried as her father set the giant tree up in a corner of the living room.

"It certainly is," her mother agreed. "Let's have supper now, and then we'll have plenty of time to trim it."

All the children helped, and soon the meal had been eaten and the dishes washed. Then everyone gathered around the tree.

"I said this would be an old-fashioned Christmas," Mr. Bobbsey reminded the twins. "In place of electric lights on the tree, we'll have large birthday candles. We are celebrating a birthday, you know."

After the colorful ornaments and strings of popcorn had been arranged among the branches, Bert and Harry helped Mr. Bobbsey attach the candles.

As Dorothy stood back to admire their handiwork, she exclaimed, "I have an idea!" Grabbing a sweater, she ran outdoors. In a few minutes she returned, her arms full of pine cones.

"Oh, that's wonderful, Dorothy!" Nan cried. "They're just what we need. We'll color them and hang them on the ends of the branches."

When this had been done, Mr. Bobbsey and the boys lighted the candles one by one. Everyone oh-ed and ah-ed.

"It's simply gorgeous!" said Dorothy.

"Now for the carols, Mommy!" Flossie pleaded.

Smiling, her mother went over to the old-fashioned spinet piano and began to play a familiar Christmas song. The children gathered around, and soon the air was full of sweet Christmas music.

As the strains of a carol died away Bert suddenly put up his hand. "Wait!" he whispered. "I hear something in the kitchen!"

At that moment Snap, who had been napping before the fireplace, stood up, his fur bristling.

He let out a low whine and started toward the kitchen.

"Let's see what it is!" Nan said, tiptoeing after the dog.

When she reached the door into the kitchen she opened it quickly. Then Nan gasped, as she saw the door in the fireplace closing stealthily!

CHAPTER XIII

THE SEARCH

WHEN Nan saw the hidden door closing, she could not repress a scream. Immediately the others crowded into the kitchen.

"What's the matter, Nan? What did you see?" her father asked quickly.

Still shaking, the girl pointed to the fireplace. "That—that door," she gasped. "I saw it close!"

Mr. Bobbsey dashed over and carefully pulled the door open. No one stood on the other side or on the steps that led down to the tunnel.

"Bring me a flashlight, Bert," his father requested.

Snap was growling softly. As soon as Mr. Bobbsey beamed the light below, the dog started down the steps. The twins' father followed. But though both went the full length of the tunnel and looked out the smokehouse door, they found no sign of an intruder, and returned.

"Nan," said her father, "perhaps you didn't close the fireplace door tightly this morning.

Then when you opened the kitchen door a little while ago maybe the draft made the other one close."

Seeing that Nan was still unconvinced and that the other children were nervous, Mrs. Bobbsey said lightly, "If there was anybody in here, we'll make sure he doesn't return this way!"

She asked Bert and Harry to move a small wooden bench in front of the fireplace door, and at her request Mr. Bobbsey swung one of the huge, heavy iron pots onto the bench.

"Now," said the twins' mother, "let's have one more carol, then hang up your stockings, and everyone go to bed. Remember, tomorrow's the big day!"

When the music ended, the children climbed the stairs drowsily and were soon fast asleep.

Flossie was the first one awake the next morning. She ran from room to room calling out, "Merry Christmas! Merry Christmas!"

Soon everyone was up and dressed and gathered in the living room. The stocking treasures were excitedly explored. There was a great laugh as Dorothy pulled out a toy lobster that instantly "pinched" her.

"Santa played a joke on you!" Freddie giggled.

Finally, at Mrs. Bobbsey's urging, the family gathered around the dining table to enjoy a breakfast of broiled ham and waffles.

"All right, children! Now for the real presents!" the twins' father called jovially.

Mrs. Bobbsey led the way to the tree where the gaily wrapped packages were piled high. For the next two hours, cries of "Just what I wanted!" and "Oh, thanks a million!" and "You remembered!" echoed through the house.

Freddie and Flossie were particularly delighted with gifts which Bert and Nan had made for them—a miniature sleigh for Flossie's doll Susie, fashioned after Mr. Carford's real one, and a wooden firehouse for Freddie's pumper.

"Is this what you and Nan were doing in the basement work shop?" Freddie asked.

"That's right," Bert replied. "Nan designed and painted them and I built them!"

"They're bee-yoo-tiful!" Flossie declared.

The hours until dinnertime were happily spent in trying on or playing with the new possessions. Then everyone sat down to a late afternoon turkey dinner, which proved to be so plentiful that Freddie had a difficult time finishing his plum pudding.

"Let's hunt for the money again," Bert suggested as they arose. "I need exercise after that dinner!"

They all agreed to continue the hunt, and Nan said, "I still think the missing money is near a mantelpiece. Remember the money disappeared from a mantelpiece. How many are there here?"

"Well," Harry began thoughtfully, "there's the living-room mantel, one in the den, and one in the kitchen."

"Let's examine the stone fireplace wall in the living room first," Nan proposed.

"There's a magnifying glass in the table drawer," Freddie announced. "That would be good to use. Real detectives do!"

"You're a wonder!" Bert exclaimed, patting his little brother on the head. "Bring the glass over here!"

Freddie hurried to the other end of the room

and returned a minute later with an old-fashioned reading glass. The children took turns
using it to examine the stones around the mantel.

Fifteen minutes later Nan exclaimed, "I think
I've found something!" She pointed to a crack
between the mantel and the stone wall. The children followed its course down the side of the fireplace until it disappeared into the floor boards.

"Give me the magnifying glass a moment,"
Bert said. "Just as I thought! See these little
marks along here? Someone has tried to pry
this crack open with a chisel!"

"That's right." Nan nodded, bending to look
again at the crack.

"This is the best clue we've found so far!"
Harry exclaimed. "Let's give it a look with the
flashlight. Maybe the money dropped down this
crack."

Nothing resembling a stack of bills could be
seen, however. Disappointed, the children continued their search of the living-room fireplace,
but by bedtime they still had had no success in
locating anything.

The next day, Sunday, was bright and clear.
Mrs. Bobbsey insisted that the hunt be given up
temporarily and that the children spend time
out of doors after a little religious service.

"Since we can't get to church today, we'll have
our own," she said.

Mrs. Bobbsey went to the spinet. Each one

chose a favorite hymn. Six were sung, then they recited the Lord's Prayer together.

"And now let's go skating," Dorothy suggested. "The wind has swept the snow off the ice."

Nan joined her, and the two girls skated back and forth, arm in arm, trying a few fancy figures, while Bert and Harry took the *Icebird* for a spin. Freddie was trying to teach his twin how to make a figure eight on the ice.

"It's easy, Flossie," he repeated. "See, you start off on one foot like this, lean to the—"

Suddenly Freddie stiffened. Pointing a shaking finger down the shoreline, he screamed:

"The Black Monster!"

Nan and Dorothy turned quickly just in time to see a dark, winged figure skim toward the shoreline and disappear into the woods some distance down the lake!

Wondering what the others were pointing at, Bert and Harry stopped the iceboat and joined them. When they heard the story, Bert said grimly, "It may have looked like a black monster, but it's human. I'm going to track him down and find out who he is!"

"I'm with you," said Harry. "Want to come along, Nan and Dorothy?" he asked. The girls accepted quickly.

"You'd better not come," Nan said to Freddie and Flossie. "How about playing up by the lodge? And tell Mother you're back."

"Okay," said Flossie. "It's too cold here any-way."

The four older children picked up their boots and, carrying them under their arms, skated off. Soon they located the trail of the strange person's skate runners near the shoreline and followed the faint traces. In a short while they came to a trampled spot on the bank where the "monster" had evidently removed his skates and donned boots.

"These tracks should be fairly easy to follow," Harry remarked.

The four children quickly changed to their boots and started inland. On and on they trudged through the woods. Some time later they came to an open field where most of the snow had been swept from the ground into a high drift on one side.

"It looks as if we've lost the bootprints," Nan said woefully.

The children made a circle of the field but failed to pick up any traces of their quarry. "Guess we'd better head back," Bert said in disappointment, and the others agreed.

"Which way did we come into this field?" Dorothy asked, looking about for their trail.

"I'm sort of turned around," Harry admitted, "but we should be able to follow our own footprints back—that is, if we can find them."

Wearily the four walked around the large

field, scanning the snow at the edge. Finally Dorothy called out, "I've found them! This is where we came in!"

Bert, Nan, and their cousins started back into the woods. For a while they trudged along silently. Then Nan groaned and sat down on a fallen tree trunk. "I'm beat!" she cried. "I didn't realize we had walked this far when we came in!"

Dorothy flopped down beside her. "I must say my legs feel like sticks," she admitted. "How about a little rest, boys?"

Bert and Harry retraced their steps to where the girls were seated. "Good idea," Bert agreed, "but it's pretty cold. I don't think we should sit here long."

"We could build a fire," Harry suggested. "If we get really warmed up, we can make better time back to the lake. Anyone have matches?"

"I do," Bert said, pulling a packet from his pocket. "I thought we might want a fire by the lake this morning, so I picked these up as we came out."

The others thought Harry's suggestion a good one and scattered out to pick up pieces of dead wood with which to build the fire. Soon a small blaze was burning.

"This would be perfect if we only had something warm to drink," Nan said. "My teeth are chattering!"

"I know!" exclaimed Dorothy. "Let's make hot chocolate!"

"Great! But how?" Harry scoffed.

"You'll see!" Dorothy replied, grinning. She went off into the woods and in a few minutes came back carrying a large can which had contained ground coffee. "I saw this under a tree we passed back there," she explained.

Dorothy washed the can out with snow, then filled it with clean snow, and placed it over the fire, which had now died down to a low flame. Next she took two chocolate bars from her pocket, broke them into small pieces, and dropped them into the melted snow.

"There!" she announced triumphantly. "Hot chocolate!"

The steaming drink tasted delicious as they passed the can from one to another. When the chocolate was gone, the children prepared to leave their little rest site. Suddenly they all stopped abruptly in their tracks. The crunching sound of snow being trampled came to their ears.

Could it be the mysterious skater returning?

CHAPTER XIV

NEW-FOUND FRIEND

HARDLY daring to breathe, the little group listened to the approaching footsteps. Then from among the trees a young man came up to them. He was of medium height and rather chunkily built.

"Hello there!" he called. "Are you lost?"

The children heaved sighs of relief, and Bert answered, "No, we're on our way back to the lake, but we're cold and tired, and decided to rest here for a while."

"It's pretty raw weather to be sitting in the woods," the stranger remarked. "My cabin isn't too far from here. Why don't you come back with me? I'll give you some lunch and show you a shortcut to the lake."

"That's very nice of you, Mr.—" Nan replied.

"I'm Dave Burdock. I guide hunting parties in these woods," the young man explained.

The twins looked at each other in amazement. *This man must be Mr. Carford's nephew!*

Noticing their glances, Dave seemed puzzled. "Do you know me? I mean, have I met you before? I don't remember—"

Nan smiled. "No, we've never met, but we do know your uncle, Mr. Carford. And your Aunt Emma Carford, too. In fact, we're spending our Christmas vacation at Snow Lodge."

At the mention of Mr. Carford's name, Dave Burdock's jaw set. Then to break the uncomfortable silence, Nan spoke up, "I think you know our father, Richard Bobbsey."

Dave smiled. "Yes, indeed. I'm glad to know you. Your father was very good to me a few years ago, and I've never forgotten it. But you're not all brothers and sisters, are you?"

The Bobbseys laughed and quickly introduced themselves and their cousins. Nan and Bert were wondering whether they should tell Dave that they knew the story of the missing money when he said: "This is funny. Here I stand talking when I should be getting you to my place where you can warm up and have something to eat. I'll bet you're hungry, aren't you?"

"We sure are!" Harry exclaimed.

"Well, follow me," Dave said. "We'll be there in no time!"

The cousins picked up their skates and trudged after the young man. In a short while they came to a tiny log cabin nestled among tall fir trees. How comforting and inviting the little house looked, with smoke curling from a big chimney!

Dave entered first. Nan and Dorothy, after knocking the snow from their boots, followed, then the boys.

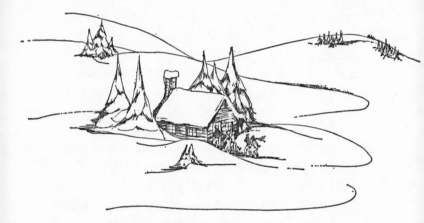

"This is terrific!" said Dorothy, looking at the cozy room and big fire.

While the children clustered in front of the burning logs, Dave went into the small kitchen. In a few minutes he returned carrying a tray on which were five bowls of steaming hot soup.

As the visitors ate hungrily, they began to talk about Snow Lodge and how much fun they were having there. Dave's face became grim, and he said through clenched teeth, "I hate that place!"

"Oh!" said Nan. "You mean because of the missing money?"

Dave looked startled. "You know about that?" he asked incredulously.

"Yes," Bert replied. "Dad told us the story, and we've been trying to find the money for you. We're sure you didn't take it!"

The young man gave a quick laugh. "Thanks for your vote of confidence," he said, "but I'm afraid my uncle doesn't share your feeling."

Nan broke in. "But I'm sure he does! He looks so sad, and I know he'd like to be friends with you again!"

"Well, I can't forget the way he treated me or the things he said," Dave went on bitterly. "I'll never speak to him again until I find that money and prove that I didn't take it!"

"Well, if that money is to be found," Harry said loyally, "my cousins can help you do it. They've solved lots of mysteries."

Dave seemed interested, so Nan and Bert explained about the searching they had already done. When they mentioned the discovery of the trap doors and the secret tunnel, Dave looked amazed.

"You must be good detectives," he remarked. "I had lived at Snow Lodge for several years before I discovered the tunnel. But I'm forgetting the rest of our lunch." He jumped up and brought plates of baked beans, bread and butter, and a pitcher of milk.

When the food had been eaten, Nan and Dorothy helped Dave wash the dishes, then they all set off through the woods. After putting the twins and their cousins on the right trail to Snow Lodge, Dave said good-by.

The children thanked him again for his kindness and promised to keep searching for the money. "We'll let you know when we find it," Bert called back over his shoulder.

"You mean *if* we find it, Bert," Harry reminded him.

"We *must* find it!" Nan exclaimed. "Everything hinges on it. We want to clear Dave's name, don't we?"

"Of course," the others chorused.

For some time they followed the winding trail through deep woods until they spotted the shoreline. Now they knew the route to the lodge.

Walking briskly, the four discussed their adventure in the woods. They had just rounded a wooded bend in the shoreline when they overtook a man and a little girl.

The man was middle-aged and dressed in a heavy lumberjacket, dungarees, and boots. The child, who appeared to be about five years old, had on a bright-red snowsuit and cap. She was sobbing.

"Oh, what's the matter?" Nan cried in sympathy. "Is there anything we can do to help?"

The man turned. "Hello there," he replied with a rueful grin. "My name's Hoke, and this is my youngest daughter Pam. Her collie pup has wandered off again. This time he seems to be really lost, and I've been trying to help her find the little fellow."

Bert introduced himself and the others and explained that they were staying at Snow Lodge.

"So you're the folks!" Mr. Hoke exclaimed. "I'm caretaker of that place. Hope you found everything in order and the rooms nice and warm." He went on, "My farm's about a mile on down the shore toward Lakeport, and I look after the lodge when nobody's staying there."

Pam glanced shyly at the children from eyes brimming with tears. "H—hello," she said finally.

"Tell us what your puppy looks like, Pam," Nan said kindly. "We'll keep an eye out for him while we're hiking. Perhaps we'll see him."

The little girl stared wistfully at Nan. "Oh, do you think you might?" she asked. "He's kind of yellowish-brown—and fat—and he has a white spot on his chest and a long white mark on his nose. His name is Chipper, and he has pretty brown eyes. I love him—" Pam looked as if she were about to burst into tears again.

"Don't you worry, honey," Nan said soothingly. "I'm sure Chipper will be found."

Waving good-by to Mr. Hoke and his little girl, the four continued to the lodge. What a welcome they received!

"Did you find the Black Monster?" Freddie asked eagerly.

"No, but we met Dave Burdock!" Nan announced.

"You did!" the others cried in astonishment.

The four children took turns telling of their meeting with Dave and their visit to his cabin.

"I feel so sorry for him, Mother!" Nan exclaimed. "He's terribly bitter and says he'll never speak to his uncle until he can prove he didn't take the money."

"Well, perhaps you children will be able to find it for him," Mrs. Bobbsey said soothingly. "I'm glad you had some lunch. We were worried about you when you didn't come back."

"I'm sorry," said Nan, and the others echoed this.

The afternoon was spent partly in playing the games they had received for Christmas and partly in further wall tapping near the fireplaces. But nothing showed up.

"Not even a tiny clue," said Dorothy sadly.

When six o'clock dinner was ready, Mr. Bobbsey carried in a huge roast beef on a platter. Nan noticed that her father was not smiling. Instead, he seemed preoccupied.

"Something's worrying Dad," Nan whispered to her twin. "I wonder what it is."

When Mr. Bobbsey pushed aside, uneaten, a piece of apple pie, everyone realized that something was amiss.

"What's wrong, Dick?" Mrs. Bobbsey finally asked. "You look so worried."

The twins' father did not answer at once. But at last he said, "I guess I'll have to tell you, because you'll find it out anyway. Snap is missing. I haven't seen him around since breakfast time!"

CHAPTER XV

A DOG HERO

STUNNED by Mr. Bobbsey's announcement that Snap was missing, Mrs. Bobbsey and the children looked at one another blankly.

"Snap missing?" Bert finally managed to repeat. "I don't understand that. He never runs away, and he's too intelligent a dog to get lost."

"It does seem strange," Nan added thoughtfully. "Unless—" She stopped for a moment and looked at Bert. "Do you suppose he went to hunt for us?"

"I'll bet that's it!" her twin exclaimed. "It would be just like Snap. Let's go into the woods and call him. If he hears our voices he'll know we're home and will come running." Bert jumped up from his chair. "May we, Mother?"

Mrs. Bobbsey nodded. In a few minutes the four older children and Mr Bobbsey were ready to go on a search. The little group set off into the dark winter night, with Bert and his father carrying flashlights. They covered the area for nearly half a mile around, calling Snap's name repeatedly, but no welcoming bark answered them.

"You're getting too cold, children," Mr. Bobbsey said finally. "We'll have to give up for tonight." So, miserable and tired, they struggled back to the lodge.

"Maybe," said Harry cheerfully, "Snap followed our trail to Dave's cabin and is there now! If he is, Dave will know from his identification tag that Snap belongs to you and will be sure to bring him back tomorrow."

"Oh, I hope you're right," Nan said.

Still somewhat anxious, though, the tired children went to bed and promptly fell asleep.

Next morning, however, Snap was still missing. Now the Bobbseys were very worried. What could have happened to their pet?

"Snap might still be at Dave's cabin," Dorothy ventured. "Maybe for some reason Dave couldn't bring him back right away."

"Then let's hike over and see," Freddie urged.

This plan was agreed to, and immediately after breakfast the twins and their cousins started off. After a brisk tramp, they reached the guide's cabin and knocked on the door. There was no answer, and they were wondering what to do next when Nan cried:

"Here he comes now!"

Dave Burdock emerged from behind the cabin bearing a load of firewood. "Good morning, children. What can I do for you today?"

Bert introduced Freddie and Flossie, then explained that they had hoped to find their dog Snap at the cabin.

Dave shook his head. "Sorry," he said. "I haven't seen any dog around here lately. But come in and get warm. Then we can look around this area."

While the children warmed their hands and feet before the blazing fire, Dave stowed away the firewood. Then he announced, "All right. Let's go!"

Together, the twins, their cousins, and their new friend scouted the woods surrounding the Burdock cabin, but they found no signs of paw prints in the snow. Nor did Snap appear when they called.

Flossie and Freddie were almost in tears. But Freddie asserted bravely, "I know we'll find Snap. We'll just keep looking until we do!"

"I'm sorry I can't help you search any more today," Dave explained, "but I have to meet some hunters in town. I'll certainly keep on the lookout for Snap on my way."

Thanking Dave for his help, the children started out again. They trudged back to the shore, then turned in the direction the older children had taken the day before.

"We mustn't forget to look for Pam's lost puppy, too," Nan reminded them as they walked along. Just then she looked up and saw Mr. Hoke and Pam coming toward her.

"Hello there!" Nan called, and introduced Freddie and Flossie. "Any luck in finding your puppy?"

Pam shook her head, and tears started to well up in her blue eyes.

"Not a trace," her father said wearily. "We're about to give up."

"We're looking for a lost dog, too," said Flossie. "He's our Snap."

"That's too bad. How long has your dog been missing?" Mr. Hoke asked.

Bert explained that they were not sure, but no one had seen him since breakfast time the previous day. He began to whistle sharply as he often did to call Snap.

Suddenly everyone's face lighted up as a muffled, joyfully barking rang through the woods.

"That's Snap!" Freddie cried excitedly, and began to run toward the sound. "Here, boy, here!" he called, as the others followed.

They traced the barking to a grove of pines some distance from the path. Bert, fearing that the dog might have met with an accident, overtook Freddie. Then he stopped abruptly.

"Here he is!" Bert cried and pointed to a deep pit in the center of the grove.

At the bottom of the hole stood Snap!

The dog's tail wagged violently the minute he spied Bert.

"He's standing over something," Nan said curiously. "Why, look, it's a puppy!"

"Chipper!" screamed Pam Hoke and almost fell into the hole in her excitement.

"Well, let's get them out," Bert urged. "Mr.

Hoke, Harry and I will climb down and pass the dogs up to you. Okay?"

The farmer agreed, and within a few moments Snap and Chipper were being hugged and petted by their young owners. Pam and Flossie were laughing and crying at the same time. After the first excitement was over, the older children tried to reconstruct the incident.

"I'll bet little Chipper fell into the hole on his travels and couldn't get out," Nan suggested.

"And Snap was on his way to find us," Bert continued, "but he heard the puppy crying and went to rescue him."

"But found he couldn't carry Chipper and climb out of the hole, too," Harry put in.

"So he stayed with the puppy to keep him safe and warm!" Dorothy exclaimed in wonder. "What a brave dog!"

Pam had heard all of this. With tears of happiness in her eyes, she threw her little arms around Snap's neck and hugged him gratefully.

"You're a real hero, Snap!" she cried. "I'll never forget that you saved my Chipper!"

Smiling, Mr. Hoke added his praise as he patted Snap. "It certainly was a fine thing to do," he said. "Snap had no way of knowing if he would ever be rescued."

Freddie shook his head. "Oh, he knew we'd be after him," he declared with assurance, "but he probably would've stayed anyway."

"Well, children," Mr. Hoke said, shaking hands with them all, "Pam and I are certainly grateful to you for being such good searchers." Then shaking Snap's paw soberly, he added, "And thank you, Snap."

The Bobbseys' pet ambled over to Chipper, licked the puppy a few times, then returned to look at the Bobbseys searchingly as if to say, "I'm starved. Let's go home!"

Laughing happily, the children said good-by to Pam and Mr. Hoke, and set off through the woods for Snow Lodge. A few minutes later they met Dave Burdock, who said he had decided not to go to town until later. He had phoned to the hunters from a house at the edge of the woods.

"I see you found Snap," he said with a smile.

Eagerly Flossie and Freddie told him the story of Snap's heroism, and Dave agreed that the dog had shown wonderful courage.

"But listen, children," he added, "you'd better hurry on back to the lodge right away. I heard a weather bureau broadcast at the house where I phoned. It predicted that a big storm soon would be moving into this area. According to the reports, it may be the worst in many years—a real old-fashioned blizzard."

"Why don't you come with us?" Nan asked. "It will be safer at Snow Lodge than in your cabin."

Dave's face clouded and he said softly, "No,

but thank you." Turning to leave, he added with a grin, "I'll be all right, but you won't if you don't hurry. Now scoot!"

Laughing, the children said good-by and set off. But by this time Freddie and Flossie were very tired after the long search for Snap. With their pet between them, they lagged farther and farther behind. Bert and Nan noticed the small twins' exhaustion, and Bert quickly offered to carry Flossie pick-a-back.

"Come on, Freddie," Harry said with a grin. "I'll give you a ride on my shoulders."

Flossie squealed with delight as her steed trotted off, and Freddie pretended to steer Harry along the path. Anxiously, Nan watched the approach of the storm. The skies grew darker and darker, and soon large flakes of snow fell lightly on the hurrying children.

Within a few minutes the wind had become a strong arm that pushed violently against the little group, making every step an effort.

Nan grabbed Snap's collar and urged him forward, as the snow thickened and swirled about them, almost obscuring the path.

At last they glimpsed the lights of the lodge about a hundred yards ahead of them. "We'd better run for it!" Bert yelled over the shrieking wind. "Hold on, kids!"

Calling on every ounce of their strength, the children raced toward Snow Lodge. But at that moment a sudden gust of howling wind struck and buffeted them about like flimsy paper dolls.

"Hang on tighter!" Bert cried to Flossie.

But the little girl wailed, "I can't, Bert! I'm slipping! Help!"

Flossie screamed as her fingers slid from her brother's shoulders and the terrible wind whipped her over backward.

CHAPTER XVI

THE BLACK MONSTER

THE INSTANT Flossie was torn from Bert's shoulders by the wind, Nan bounded forward to aid the little girl. Bracing herself against the wind, she caught Flossie's snowsuit, halting her backward tumble. A second later, Bert caught up his small sister in his arms and staggered toward the lodge.

Harry, with Freddie still on his shoulders, reached the house first and threw open the door. Nan and Dorothy rushed in behind him.

"Hurry!" the children cried over the howling wind, watching fearfully as Bert struggled up the steps to the door.

Quickly the older girls lifted Flossie from Bert's grasp and set her down. Snap, who had waited to see that everyone was safely inside, sprang through the opening at the last moment.

Mr. and Mrs. Bobbsey, who had hastened to

meet the children, pushed on the door together and finally managed to close it. Snow-covered and exhausted, the children were glad to remove their snowsuits and lie on the floor before a roaring fire in the living-room hearth.

Mrs. Bobbsey served a late lunch there, and soon all the children were napping. Later, they told Mr. and Mrs. Bobbsey about Snap's act of heroism and mentioned the fact that Dave Burdock had warned them about the blizzard and had perhaps saved them from becoming lost in the storm.

"We asked him to come back with us to Snow Lodge," Nan added. "But he wouldn't."

Mr. Bobbsey nodded sadly. "It's too bad that Dave is so resentful. He and Mr. Carford could be living here right now, if only he'd forgive and forget."

Bert stirred restlessly in his chair. "If we could find the money, the whole thing would be straightened out."

He started a new hunt, joined by the other children. But at bedtime they stopped. Not a clue had turned up.

By morning the storm had abated entirely, and the sun was out again.

"How about going over to Dave's cabin and seeing if he's all right?" Bert proposed as they finished breakfast. "*Maybe* we can talk him into forgiving his uncle."

"Oh, yes!" Dorothy agreed. "And I have an idea!"

"What's that?"

"Let's go out by way of the tunnel. We can take flashlights and examine it as we go along. Perhaps we can find out what it was used for!"

In a few minutes, bundled up against the cold and armed with lights, they stepped through the secret door in the kitchen fireplace. They took

up their usual order with Bert in the lead, then Dorothy, Flossie, Nan, Freddie, and Harry bringing up the rear.

As they walked slowly through the tunnel, flashing their lights over the walls and ceiling, they realized for the first time that the passage-way was about three feet wide and high enough to permit a tall man to walk upright. The walls and ceiling were of brick, but the floor was dirt.

"This tunnel certainly looks as if it had been

made for a special purpose," Bert observed. "I wonder how old it is."

"It's still scary," Flossie put in, her voice trembling a little.

Just then Bert bent forward so suddenly that Dorothy almost fell over him. When he stood up, Bert held a small object in his hand.

"What did you find?" Nan asked, pressing forward to see.

"A black button! And I don't think it's been here very long!" Bert turned it over in his fingers. The button was still shiny and dry.

"Someone *has* been in here lately!" Nan exclaimed. "Remember Christmas Eve? It wasn't the wind that made that door close—it was a person!"

"But why would anyone use this tunnel now?" Dorothy questioned.

"I don't know, but let's keep our eyes open for anything else new in here," Nan replied.

But they reached the stairs and trap door to the old smokehouse without finding another clue to the mysterious intruder.

"Ooo, I'm glad to be out of there!" Flossie exclaimed as they emerged into the bright sunlight. "Now let's go see Mr. Burdock!"

The six children trudged through the newly fallen snow for fifteen minutes or so until they came within sight of Dave Burdock's cabin nestled among the trees. A wisp of smoke curled up from the chimney.

"Dave must be all right," Dorothy observed. "He has a fire going."

They hurried forward, and Bert knocked on the door. There was no reply. He pounded louder. Still no answer.

"Maybe he's gone into town," Freddie said.

"Or he could be hurt and not be able to come to the door," Flossie said, her chin beginning to quiver.

"I think we should go in if the door's unlocked," Nan said firmly. "Try it, Bert."

The door swung open with Bert's push, and the children stepped inside. The room was empty.

"Perhaps he's in the kitchen," Harry said, opening that door. But Dave was not there.

"Let's sit down and wait for him," Nan proposed. "He'll probably be back soon." She walked over to the camp bed, then stopped in surprise.

"Look!" she cried, pulling something from between the cot and the wall.

It was a black cape!

"That's what the Black Monster wears!" Freddie cried out.

"Dave Burdock is the Black Monster?" Dorothy asked unbelievingly.

The children were too shocked to speak for a few minutes, and sat in gloomy silence.

Finally Bert said, "The top button on the cape is missing." From his pocket he took the button he had picked up in the tunnel of Snow Lodge. It matched the ones on the cape exactly!

"Dave has been spying on us. But why?"

"But Mr. Carford's nephew *can't* be the Black Monster!" Nan said in a shocked tone.

"Sure, he is," said Dorothy indignantly.

At this moment Nan happened to look out the window. Dave Burdock and another man, wearing a dark blue ski cap and jacket, were coming. Soon they walked into the cabin.

"Well, visitors," Dave said cheerily. "Glad to see you."

The children did not smile, and Freddie piped up, "You're the Black Monster!"

"What!" Dave exclaimed.

"This is the cape you wear to hide under," Harry told him, holding it up.

Dave Burdock stared, speechless. "I never saw that before in my life." He turned to speak to the man he had brought along. "Will, do you—"

But Will was not there. He was streaking up the path. Like a shot, Bert, Harry, and Dave Burdock were after him. The race was short, and Will was captured. He was marched back to the cabin.

"Now suppose you all tell me what this is about," Dave demanded.

Will was silent, so Bert told about the rumpus at Mr. Carford's, the warning note to the Bobbsey twins, and the secret stranger visiting Snow Lodge secretly.

"Okay, I'll talk," said Will, who gave his last name as Beck, a woodsman. "I've known old

Mr. Carford and Dave here for a long time. I wanted to see Dave cleared, so I've been searching in the lodge a long time for that money.

"When I heard from the Hokes that you folks were coming up—well, I didn't want you snooping around and maybe finding it."

As Will paused, Bert interrupted. "What difference does it make who finds the money so long as Mr. Carford gets it?"

"He don't deserve it!" Will blustered.

"You mean you were going to keep it?" Harry burst out.

"I was going to share it with Dave here," Will answered. "He's my friend. He let me sleep here when I got caught in the blizzard."

"But the money, if it's found, belongs to my uncle," Dave insisted.

"That mean old codger? Bah!" Will scoffed.

"He's very kind—a regular Santa Claus," Nan spoke up.

Dorothy asked, "Why did you call yourself the Black Monster and wear the cape?"

"To keep folks from seeing my face and to scare you if I could," Will explained. Clasping and unclasping his hands nervously, the woodsman continued:

"My father used to wear this cape in the woods when it was cold, so I hit upon the idea of putting it on and calling myself the Black Monster. Dave here didn't know I had it." Will also admitted shamefacedly that he had cut the mainsheet on Bert's iceboat.

"You probably thought that wouldn't be serious," Harry spoke up. "But the mainsheet gave way in the midst of a storm. The *Icebird* turned over, and we were all thrown out!"

Will looked distressed. "I sure am sorry for that," he said, shaking his head. "I guess I got kind of excited trying to worry you Bobbseys so you'd go back home." He also admitted telephoning the family's home and pretending to be a newspaperman to find out when the Bobbseys would arrive at Snow Lodge. And Will, not Danny, had frightened Mr. Carford's chickens.

Dave Burdock stood up. "I'm amazed at you, Will Beck. You've always been honest and straightforward. I'm sure this has been a lesson to you."

"Yes," the woodsman admitted. "And it took a bunch of children to teach me." Without another word he picked up his cape, took the loose button from Bert, and stalked out the door.

Flossie rushed over to Dave Burdock and jumped into his arms. "Oh, I'm so glad you weren't the Black Monster! Now everything's just bee-yoo-ti-ful!"

The guide smiled at her. "I think maybe you children have taught me a lesson, too. At least, I have a lot to mull over."

There was a long pause. Finally Freddie spoke up. "I'm glad nobody mean found the money that got lost at Snow Lodge. Now we can hunt harder and harder!"

CHAPTER XVII

SNOWBOUND

"DON'T tell me we're going to have another snowstorm!" Dorothy said as she and Harry and the twins trudged toward home. "Snow Lodge is certainly well named!"

The sky had darkened, and fine flakes of snow drifted down. By the time the children reached the house the snow was falling heavily and showed no signs of stopping. At once the twins and their cousins told about their morning at Dave Burdock's cabin.

"It's an amazing story," Mr. Bobbsey said, "and I'm glad the mystery is solved." He laughed. "You children almost had me believing there *was* a black monster."

The room had become so dim from the storm outside that Mrs. Bobbsey snapped on the lights. Now they suddenly went out.

"Oh, oh!" Bert exclaimed. "Power failure!"

Mr. Bobbsey jumped up and peered out a window. "The weight of the snow has torn the wires loose," he reported. "We'll be without electricity for quite a while, I'm afraid!"

"Ooh!" Flossie gasped, then said, "We can do everything by candlelight. I love that!"

Candles were lighted, but Mr. Bobbsey also found some kerosene lamps and a large can of kerosene in the cellar. Soon the rooms were cozy with the soft glow of their light.

"I see now," Mrs. Bobbsey remarked, "why Mr. Carford left the old wood-burning stove in the kitchen when he installed a modern electric range. Otherwise how would I be able to cook hot meals or heat water until the power comes back on?"

In the afternoon the children became restless. They had searched carefully all over the first floor of the lodge and had not found the money. "We might try the attic," Nan suggested, "although I don't see how it could be there."

Nevertheless, with Bert and Harry each carrying a lantern, the six children mounted the stairs to the attic.

After peering around for a few minutes, Flossie suddenly exclaimed, "Oh Nan! We forgot! Remember Mr. Carford told us we could play with the things in these trunks!"

"Of course!" Nan replied. "Let's see what's in them."

Raising the lid of the nearest trunk, she pulled out old-fashioned suits and dresses, and even high-topped shoes with little tassels dangling from them.

"What fun!" Dorothy cried. "Let's all dress up!"

The boys entered into the spirit of the masquerade and pulled out long, tight trousers and ruffled shirts. Soon each child had an armful of clothes, and they dashed down to the bedrooms to change.

Mr. and Mrs. Bobbsey were reading in front of the fire when the procession came down the stairs. "Look, Mother!" Nan cried. "We're giving a style show!"

Nan and Dorothy wore crinolines which swayed as they walked, showing white ruffled pantalets. Flossie had on a long green skirt which she had tied up under her arms with a wide red sash. Freddie wore cowboy chaps and a toy lariat draped from his belt. The older boys had put on the long trousers and tail coats which almost reached the floor.

The twins' parents burst into shouts of laughter. "That's quite a mixture of styles!" Mr. Bobbsey gasped when he could speak.

"Oh! I wish I could take your pictures!" Mrs. Bobbsey exclaimed between chuckles.

Pleased with the impression they had made, the children paraded around the room. Then

Nan stopped in front of her mother. "Why don't we have a party this evening?" she begged. "We have the costumes, and we should make it a special occasion since we're marooned in a snowstorm with no electricity!"

Mrs. Bobbsey laughed. "I agree that it is a good night for a party. What kind do you want to have?"

"You let us plan it, Aunt Mary," Dorothy replied. "You won't have to do anything but come and have a good time."

"And Freddie and I can stay up late until the end of the party," Flossie pleaded.

"Well, if you and Freddie will go now and take naps, maybe that can be arranged," Mr. Bobbsey said with a wink at his wife.

For the remainder of the afternoon the six children forgot about the storm outside. The small twins were too excited to nap for long and soon were dashing about helping Nan, Bert, and their cousins as they prepared for the big celebration.

Nan and Dorothy made small party sandwiches and baked cupcakes in the old-fashioned stove. Bert and Harry planned some skits and games. Freddie ran back up into the attic and after a search discovered some noisemakers in one of the trunks and a lot of colored tissue paper. He helped Flossie make fancy hats from the paper.

The small twins were whispering excitedly in a corner when Dorothy came into the living room. "What are you two imps planning?" she asked.

"Oh—uh—nothing," Freddie replied evasively. Then, giggling, he and Flossie ran off up the stairs.

By the time Mrs. Bobbsey called them for the

evening meal, everything was in readiness. At the table all eight of the Snow Lodge guests were in a festive mood.

When dinner was over and the dishes washed, Mr. and Mrs. Bobbsey suddenly disappeared without saying a word to anyone.

"Harry," Bert called to his cousin, who had been drying dishes in the kitchen, "come help me lay a big, roaring fire in the living room. The one we had this afternoon is all ashes."

"The rest of us will get things out for the skits and games," Nan volunteered.

Soon everything was ready, and the children were eager to begin the celebration.

"But where are Aunt Mary and Uncle Dick?" Dorothy asked, as the young people assembled in the living room.

Suddenly there was a sound on the steps. The children rushed into the hall. Coming down the stairs arm in arm, were two quaintly dressed people.

"Surprise!" Mr. and Mrs. Bobbsey cried out.

Then Mrs. Bobbsey added, "Don't you recognize us? We thought we should dress formally for your party."

"But where did you get those costumes?" Nan wanted to know. "You look like pictures of the people in the last century."

The twins' mother wore a beautiful, long flowing gown of pale blue silk with huge puffed sleeves and creamy lace at the neck. The crown of her large pink hat was wreathed with vari-colored flowers.

Mr. Bobbsey had on narrow striped trousers, a gold brocaded vest, and a long black jacket. In his right hand he carried a tall silk hat and a gold-handled cane.

"Oh," Nan breathed, "you look simply wonderful!"

"Daddy, you're bee-yoo-ti-ful!" Flossie cried, clasping her hands together in admiration.

Mr. and Mrs. Bobbsey were pleased with the reception they had received. "You looked so cute in your costumes," Mrs. Bobbsey explained, "that Daddy and I decided to investigate those trunks, too. I think we found the best one!"

The evening's gaiety started with playing charades. For Flossie's and Freddie's sakes the words were kept simple. When the score was added, it was found that Mrs. Bobbsey's team, consisting of Dorothy, Bert, and Freddie, were the winners. The other side had failed to guess "cobweb" and "blanket."

"Before we start the skits," Freddie piped up, "how about the refreshments? I know I can play my part better if my tummy is full."

"All right, my little fat fireman," his father teased him. The dainty sandwiches and gaily decorated cupcakes were brought in by Nan and Dorothy. Flossie passed out the noisemakers, and

Freddie put a fancy hat on each of the children. What a din as four horns and four rattles were used at once!

Freddie heaped his plate high and, with Flossie following him, headed for a corner of the living room. Pillows had been arranged there in front of a makeshift stage where the skits were to be held, so he and Flossie sat down on them to enjoy their refreshments.

The rest of the party gathered around the fireplace, eating and chatting gaily. It was some time before Mrs. Bobbsey realized that the small twins had become very quiet.

She glanced in the direction of the stage and there on the pillows lay Freddie and Flossie—fast asleep! The little boy still clutched a half-eaten cupcake in his chubby hand.

"Let's carry them up to bed, Dick," Mrs. Bobbsey suggested. "I was afraid they wouldn't be able to stay awake." She and Mr. Bobbsey went to pick up their small twins.

As Freddie was lifted from the pillows he awoke with a start. "Oh, hi, Daddy!" he said, rubbing his eyes. "We're all ready for the skits."

"Don't you think the skits can wait until tomorrow?" his father asked. "You're pretty sleepy and it's very late."

"Please no, Daddy. I wasn't really asleep," Freddie replied groggily. "Flossie and I have a very special skit we just have to do."

"Well, all right," his father agreed. "But after that you must go to bed."

Mrs. Bobbsey nodded approval, and the two children dashed out of the room.

"What is this skit that's so important?" Mr. Bobbsey asked the other children.

"We don't know, Dad," Bert answered. "It's something they planned themselves and wouldn't tell us about."

"I saw Freddie making a paste of flour and water," Harry said, grinning.

"And Flossie came to me and asked me to tie two big red hair ribbons together," Nan added.

"What on earth can they be up to?" Mrs. Bobbsey wondered aloud.

In a few minutes the waiting group heard steps on the stairs and Freddie called, "Okay, we're ready!"

Mr. and Mrs. Bobbsey and the four older children made themselves comfortable in front of the stage. Then Flossie cried, "Here we come!"

The audience turned toward the doorway. What a sight they saw!

First came Flossie, dressed only in her underwear, with a huge red ribbon tied in a bow on her hip and circling the opposite shoulder.

Behind Flossie came Freddie. He had pasted cotton together with flour and water to make a beard, and his small body was wrapped in a large sheet, held together at the waist by a huge safety pin. In one hand, he carried a small sickle, and in the other, an hourglass eggtimer.

The living room rang with laughter, and it was easy to see that Freddie and Flossie were finding it hard to keep from giggling, too.

"Do you know who we are?" Freddie asked eagerly.

"Snow White and Prince Charming?" his father suggested.

Flossie giggled. "Oh, Daddy! You're teasing us!" she protested.

"Jack and Jill?" Bert suggested.

"I guess we'll have to tell them!" Flossie said with a make-believe sigh.

"I'm Father Time," Freddie explained. "And Flossie's Baby New Year!"

"You see, we decided not to wait for New Year's Eve," Flossie added, her blue eyes sparkling.

"We really knew who you were meant to be all the time," Mrs. Bobbsey said reassuringly. "Your skit was very good."

The older children gathered around the small twins to congratulate them and admire the costumes. Then suddenly came a loud *snap,* like the crack of a giant whip. The merrymakers looked at one another fearfully.

"Wh-what's that?" Flossie whispered, clutching Nan's hand.

The next second a thundering crash filled the room, and Snow Lodge seemed to shudder on its foundation!

CHAPTER XVIII

WONDERFUL DISCOVERY

AS SNOW LODGE shook under the violent impact, the Bobbsey family and their visitors huddled together and looked around the room. Bits of mortar had sprayed from the fireplace onto the floor. From the den snowflakes and wind blew into the room.

"I think a tree must have fallen on the den," the twins' father said. "The weight of all the snow on its branches probably weakened it, and the wind toppled it over."

The group rushed to the entrance of the den. A scene of ruin confronted them. As Mr. Bobbsey had guessed, a huge old tree had fallen through the roof, its topmost branches blocking the door from the living room. Snow-laden boughs poked through the demolished roof and lay heavily on the crushed furniture.

Even the old den fireplace had been badly damaged by the crash. The long, heavy mantelpiece lay on the floor, knocked there by the impact of the falling tree. Wind howled. Snow swirled into the living room. A blast of cold air blew in.

"Bert! Harry! Quick!" Mr. Bobbsey said. "We must shut off this room. It seems to be the only part of the lodge that was hit, so if we can close the door, we shouldn't be too uncomfortable in the rest of the house."

"I'll get an axe, Dad," Bert offered, and raced to the cellar.

When he returned a few minutes later, Harry and Mr. Bobbsey had moved aside some of the smaller branches of the tree. At once Bert began chopping, and before long a large enough piece of the tree trunk had been hacked away to allow the door to be closed.

At last it was latched, but the sagging frame prevented a tight fit. Harry ran to the kitchen for rags and newspapers to stuff around the frame and within a few minutes the demolished room was fairly well sealed off.

Meanwhile the others were busy sweeping up mortar and small pieces of stone which had fallen from the fireplace wall in the living room. When the chore was concluded, Mrs. Bobbsey said everyone should go to bed.

"You're right," the twins' father agreed.

"Boy, what a day of excitement!" Harry exclaimed.

Freddie awoke first next morning, delighted to find sunshine filtering through the snow-framed windows. One toot on his horn and the whole family was aroused! After a hasty breakfast, everyone went to the den to inspect the damage by daylight.

"What a mess!" Freddie exclaimed, voicing the unanimous opinion.

Mr. Bobbsey organized work crews to start the clean-up of debris from the storm. While he and Bert were sawing off the tree limbs protruding into the den, the other children were to shovel snow, making paths both to the woodpile and the road.

By midmorning, both tasks were accomplished and Nan, Bert, Harry, and Dorothy helped carry the tree limbs outside. Their removal showed that the roof and the den fireplace would need extensive repairs and that some of the furniture would have to be replaced.

"We'd better carry the good furniture and books and knickknacks into the other rooms," Nan suggested.

Willingly all hands set to work, picking up and carrying the articles away. Nan, busy near the fireplace wall, suddenly peered into a crack of loosened mortar back of where the mantelpiece had been, and gave a startled gasp.

"Oh, come here quick, everybody!" she called. "There's something green in here. Do you supposed it could be—"

Nan did not need to finish the sentence. Instantly, the other children dashed forward. Bert, Harry, and Dorothy, as well as Nan, tried to reach down into the crack, but their hands were too large.

"You try it, Floss," Bert suggested and held her up.

Flossie's small hand slid easily into the crack. She cried out, "I feel something!"

The little girl rummaged about a second more, then pulled out a ragged, dust-covered stack of green papers. When it was brushed off and opened, the children stared in astonishment.

The stack contained several bills, all of large denominations!

Too excited to say a word, the children dashed into the living room where Mr. and Mrs. Bobbsey were rearranging furniture to accommodate the new pieces.

"We've found it!" Bert finally managed to cry as Flossie waved the bills before her parents. "The missing money! See, Dave didn't steal it! And that fellow Will didn't find it!"

Quickly Mr. Bobbsey counted the money. Then, beaming at the children, he exclaimed, "The exact amount that Mr. Carford said he lost that day from the mantel is here! It fell down behind and got wedged out of sight, I suppose."

"And it was there all the time!" Nan exclaimed. "Oh, poor Dave! And poor Mr. Carford!"

For the next hour Snow Lodge was a scene of happy pandemonium.

"Actually," said Nan excitedly, "the storm and the falling tree were blessings in disguise. In all these years no one found the money, but Old Man Snowstorm fixed that!"

"Didn't we have luck!" Freddie exclaimed.

Mrs. Bobbsey smiled at the children proudly. "A little luck and some good detecting," she said. "If you hadn't been so watchful, Nan, you might never have noticed the money at all. It probably would have stayed right in that crack and been covered over by a new mantel!"

"Dad," said Bert, "shouldn't we get word to Dave and Mr. Carford right away?"

"Yes. Dave first."

As they discussed hiking to Dave's cabin, a knock came on the back door.

"I'll get it," Freddie offered and scampered to the kitchen. Opening the door, he cried out, "It's Dave!"

Everyone hurried to greet him and all talked at once about the wonderful find. For a moment Dave Burdock was too surprised to utter a word. Choked with emotion, he followed the Bobbseys into the living room.

Finally he managed to say, "I just don't know how to thank you folks. You can't imagine how much this means to me to have my name cleared!"

"Don't you think we should let Mr. Carford know right away that the money has been found, Dad?" Nan suggested.

"I certainly do," he agreed. "Dave, is there any chance of getting through to Lakeport?"

Dave replied that he had come over to Snow Lodge not only to see if everyone was safe, but also to tell the Bobbseys about the road. The snowplow had managed to clear it, and the electric power would be restored before long.

"I'll start for Lakeport now," Mr. Bobbsey said.

Bert spoke up. "Dad, how about bringing Mr. Carford back with you and we can have a party to celebrate?"

His suggestion was greeted with enthusiasm, and the twins' father started off. Dave remained at the lodge to help cut and bring in wood which was needed.

The afternoon passed quickly and happily. Mrs. Bobbsey and the children tidied the lodge and even made some paper decorations for the dinner table. Shortly before dark, the electric power came back on, and the kerosene lamps were returned to the basement. Mrs. Bobbsey bustled about the kitchen preparing dinner.

Finally Mr. Bobbsey arrived with Mr. Carford. The elderly man strode up to his nephew with hand extended.

"Dave," he said, his voice trembling, "I hope you can forgive me for my unjust accusation. For some time now I've felt you couldn't have been guilty, but you refused to see me or talk to me. Now that the mystery has been solved, can't we be friends again?"

Dave flushed in embarrassment as he grasped his uncle's hand. "It's what I've hoped for, sir," he said, "but I wanted you to be absolutely sure!"

Everyone beamed as they sat down to dinner. Mr. Carford looked around, a broad smile on his lined face. "This is the nicest way I know of to end an old year. And we owe it all to the Bobbseys!" Then he looked sad as he added, "Perhaps this will be a lesson to you young ones. Never accuse anyone of wrongdoing unless you know it is true!"

The children were thoughtful for a minute, remembering how they had accused Danny wrongly, then promised to take his advice.

As they ate, the twins and their cousins eagerly recounted their various adventures to Mr. Carford. Presently Nan asked him if he knew about the tunnel leading from the kitchen to the old smokehouse.

"Yes, I remember I used to play in it sometimes when I was a child. But to tell the truth, I'd forgotten all about it over the years."

"Have you any idea how old the tunnel is?" Bert asked. "Or what it was used for?"

Mr. Carford thought for a moment, then replied, "I can't give you any exact dates, but I should say it's close to two hundred years old. This house was put up before the American Revolution. The farmer who built it probably used the tunnel to get from the kitchen to the smokehouse during the heavy snows."

"Is that all it was used for?" Flossie asked, disappointed that the tunnel did not have a more mysterious story.

Mr. Carford smiled. "Well, there are rumors that the tunnel was used to hide American soldiers during the Revolutionary War."

"How exciting!" Nan cried. "Just think! Perhaps one of the Bobbsey twins' ancestors hid down there!"

"Could be," Mr. Carford replied. "The English captured this area early in the war and imprisoned many American soldiers nearby. Folks say some managed to escape from time to time and used the old tunnel as a hideaway for a few weeks.

"Then," he continued, "when the hue and cry had died down a bit, the soldiers would slip back to their own army to fight again."

This exciting information led to much speculation about the part the old tunnel might have played in winning the Revolutionary War.

Later, Mrs. Bobbsey smiled at Mr. Carford and said, "Actually, the children have cleared up three mysteries during our stay here at Snow Lodge."

"That's right," Dorothy agreed. "The secret tunnel—"

"And the Black Monster mystery," Bert said with a wink at Dave.

"And the case of the missing money," Nan added.

"Wow!" Freddie exclaimed. "We should go into the mystery-solving business! When we get home let's hang a sign on our front door:

THE BOBBSEY TWINS' DETECTIVE AGENCY, UNLIMITED!"

ORDER FORM

BOBBSEY TWINS ADVENTURE SERIES

Now that you've met the Bobbsey Twins, we're sure you'll want to "accompany" them on other exciting adventures. So for your convenience, we've enclosed this handy order form.

47 TITLES AT YOUR BOOKSELLER OR COMPLETE AND MAIL THIS HANDY COUPON TO:

GROSSET & DUNLAP, INC.
P.O. Box 941, Madison Square Post Office, New York, N.Y. 10010
Please send me the Bobbsey Twins Adventure Book(s) checked below @ $2.50 each, plus 25¢ *per book* postage and handling. My check or money order for $_____ is enclosed.

☐ 1. Of Lakeport	8001-X	☐ 27. Solve A Mystery 8027-3
☐ 2. Adventure in the Country	8002-8	☐ 47. At Big Bear Pond 8047-8
☐ 3. Secret at the Seashore	8003-6	☐ 48. On A Bicycle Trip 8048-6
☐ 4. Mystery at School	8004-4	☐ 49. Own Little Ferryboat 8049-4
☐ 5. At Snow Lodge	8005-2	☐ 50. At Pilgrim Rock 8050-8
☐ 6. On A Houseboat	8006-0	☐ 51. Forest Adventure 8051-6
☐ 7. Mystery at Meadowbrook	8007-9	☐ 52. At London Tower 8052-4
☐ 8. Big Adventure at Home	8008-7	☐ 53. In the Mystery Cave 8053-2
☐ 9. Search in the Great City	8009-5	☐ 54. In Volcano Land 8054-0
☐ 10. On Blueberry Island	8010-9	☐ 55. And the Goldfish Mystery 8055-9
☐ 11. Mystery on the Deep Blue Sea	8011-7	☐ 56. And the Big River Mystery 8056-7
☐ 12. Adventure in Washington	8012-5	☐ 57. The Greek Hat Mystery 8057-5
☐ 13. Visit to the Great West	8013-3	☐ 58. Search for the Green Rooster 8058-3
☐ 14. And the Cedar Camp Mystery	8014-1	☐ 59. And Their Camel Adventure 8059-1
☐ 15. And the County Fair Mystery	8015-X	☐ 60. Mystery of the King's Puppet 8060-S
☐ 16. Camping Out	8016-8	☐ 61. Secret of Candy Castle 8061-3
☐ 17. Adventures With Baby May	8017-6	☐ 62. And the Doodlebug Mystery 8062-1
☐ 18. And the Play House Secret	8018-4	☐ 63. And the Talking Fox Mystery 8063-X
☐ 19. And the Four-Leaf Clover Mystery	8019-2	☐ 64. The Red, White and Blue Mystery 8064-8
☐ 20. The Mystery at Cherry Corners	8020-6	☐ 65. Dr. Funnybone's Secret 8065-6
☐ 24. Wonderful Winter Secret	8024-9	☐ 66. The Tagalong Giraffe 8066-4
☐ 25. And the Circus Surprise	8025-7	☐ 67. And the Flying Clown 8067-2
		☐ 68. On The Sun-Moon Cruise 8068-0
		☐ 69 The Freedom Bell Mystery 8069-9
		☐ 70. And the Smoky Mountain Mystery 8070-2

SHIP TO:

NAME _____
(please print)

ADDRESS _____

CITY _____ STATE _____ ZIP _____

Printed in U.S.A.